Moon of
Two Dark Horses

Sally M. Keehn

A Yearling Book

Published by
Bantam Doubleday Dell Books for Young Readers
a division of
Bantam Doubleday Dell Publishing Group, Inc.
1540 Broadway
New York, New York 10036

The term "Americans" is used throughout this novel to refer to the white settlers who rebelled against the British king. In recorded speeches, the Native Americans of 1776 often referred to the rebels by this name.

ISBN: 0-440-41287-0

Reprinted by arrangement with Philomel Books, a division of The Putnam & Grosset Group

Printed in the United States of America

September 1997

10 9 8 7 6 5 4 3 2 1

OPM

For warm lights in my wilderness—
my mother, Mary Giffen Miller,
and
my editor, Patricia Lee Gauch

—S.K.

Before the United States was born, a federation of tribes known as the Iroquois League was considered the most powerful group of Native Americans on the continent. By 1776, the year this novel opens, six tribes composed the League: the Mohawks, Senecas, Oneidas, Cayugas, Tuscaroras, and Onondagas. All were located in what is now central New York State. This was an important geographical location, for the Iroquois formed a barrier against white advancement northward into Canada and controlled access to important waterways and Indian paths.

At the southern boundary of Iroquois territory lived a group of Delawares (a tribe that had gradually been pushed inland from the Atlantic seacoast). Their village stood along the Susquehanna River at the New York-Pennsylvania border. Here, the Delawares held hands with their Iroquois "uncles" to the north and with white settlers to the south.

When the Revolutionary War broke out and the American colonies separated from the British king, both sides told the Iroquois and their Delaware "nephews" to take no part. But as the fighting escalated, the white men's armies realized the Native Americans would make formidable allies. Each began to pressure the tribes into joining their side.

PROLOGUE

*A*uween *guntschimgun?* Who called you? Why do you stand there, arms crossed, beneath my ash tree? Go away! Too many times I've tried to tell my story. No one listens. They glance at the branch on which I sit, but their eyes see only trembling leaves. They cock their heads. Then they laugh at themselves, believing their ears have fooled them—hearing a boy's voice in the wind.

If they would see and listen with their hearts, they would know that I, Coshmoo, am here. They'd sit beneath my ash tree as you are doing now. They'd face west with legs crossed and hands resting in their laps. They'd listen to me the way I listened to Broken Stone tell his stories when I was among the breathing.

But no. Too full of questions, they wouldn't listen. They'd ask, "Where does this voice come from? The wind? Is it the echo of a wolf's howl? The clicking of bones? Whispers from a grave?"

Look down into the valley. See that arrowhead of

1

land where the Chemung River merges with the Susquehanna? That's Tioga Point. It guards the entrance to the Forbidden Path, which leads to Iroquois country. My village stretched along the riverbanks, across from the meeting of waters at Tioga. Here my people, the Delawares, held out their hands to both the Indian and the white man.

I know, you see only blackened rubble. Charred deerskins stretched on drying racks. The burned and broken shells of three canoes. But once my village had seventy log and plank houses, built in the white man's way. It had fields of cattle, and orchards red with apples!

I see the questions in your eyes. You want to know what happened to this village that was as fine as any white man's town. I don't know if I can tell you, but I'll try.

I will start with Daniel. He's the reason I must tell a story full of spirits, bones, and dreams.

Whatever I may say, you must promise not to sigh. Not for my people, nor for me. No one can take Tioga Point from us. We are the wind, teasing the clouds above it. Our spirits sing the rivers' songs and our souls enrich the earth. An Ancient Warrior's bones still dance among these hills. At night, you can hear them clicking.

CHAPTER
I

SPRING 1776

If he swims closer, grab his tail," Daniel whispered. His arm brushed against mine as we crouched together on a sun-baked rock. In the shallow water just below, Red Eye swam back and forth, protecting the round nest he'd fanned out of gravel in the river bottom. He was not a big fish, but he was wily. For more than five long breaths, I'd dangled my hand in chilly water, hoping he'd think it was a rock or log and brush against it. Then I'd grab him. But Red Eye kept to his wider circle and did not come near.

I inched myself over the edge of the rock until my fingers touched the nest. A blacksmith's hammer clanged and Red Eye darted, hiding among sunken branches.

"He'll come back," Daniel signed.

The Susquehanna River, which snaked through the land Daniel called Pennsylvania, lapped the rock that held us. Soon, the river would teem with fish. Not with Red Eyes, but with shad. At the time the shadbush bloomed, these mighty fish fought currents to swim north past Daniel's farm to my village and beyond to give birth to their young. I sensed the coming of these shad. The wind and river sang it.

"Look! Red Eye's peeking out at us," Daniel whispered, his breath warm against my cheek.

I caught passing glints of two red eyes and the pale gray of a belly weaving in and out of branches. Coming closer now. A little Red Eye moving in and out of the watery reflection of two faces. Mine was round, with high cheekbones, dark eyes, and a lick of hair no amount of bear grease could flatten. Daniel's had a pointed chin, blue eyes, and light brown hair that stood up just like mine.

Daniel's watery face grinned at me. It felt good to see his grin again. Three moons was too long for friends to be apart.

Red Eye's mouth opened and closed as he slowly circled my hand. Nearer. Nearer.

"Now!" Daniel whispered.

I held my breath and lunged. I felt Red Eye's slick, firm body between my palm and fingers. Felt his flapping tail. Then . . . nothing but cold water and gritty sand.

"I had him!" I looked at my empty hand. I couldn't believe that Red Eye had escaped. I stared at the water, all cloudy with silt and gravel. Water lapped happily against the rock, as if the Susquehanna didn't care that I'd caught a fish and lost it.

"A Red Eye never abandons his nest. He'll return." Daniel slipped his hand into the water, too, and our reflected faces shimmered. I liked the way these faces seemed to touch, then merge, each for a moment a part of the other.

Lowanachen, the north wind, rippled our reflections. Lowanachen rustled through the willows that flanked us. It played with the scent of coming shad, newly budded trees, and the rich decay of fallen leaves.

"Coshmoo." Daniel's hushed voice was like the wind, whispering my name. "Your cousin, Flying Wolf."

Instinctively, we flattened ourselves against the rock. Our dangling hands became a part of the river bottom; our arms, slim brown logs. From our concealing cave of rock and willows, we watched in silence as Flying Wolf eased his canoe around a bend in the far side of the river. A spear jutted out from the bow. If I'd heaved a stone with all my might, I could have hit my cousin. He was that close to us.

"What's he doing here?" Daniel said.

"Hunting eel," I replied, although I knew it was more than this. Flying Wolf could catch eel six miles upriver at my village.

His canoe edged around a bend and disappeared between a wooded island and the shore. Daniel and I laughed softly as we caught ourselves sighing together in relief at not being seen.

"When will he return to the land of the Senecas?" Daniel said.

"Once the shad have finished running," I replied.

Every spring, Flying Wolf's village, mostly Senecas, traveled south to Tioga Point to net shad with us. Every spring, we held a contest to see who could catch the most fish. Every spring, it seemed, my boastful cousin would win.

"I hope the shad spawn soon," Daniel said.

"I do, too. After Flying Wolf's been with us several nights, even the hungry dogs keep away. He's even louder and more boastful than he used to be, because he has a musket now." I hoped Daniel would say that his father had a musket, as well. That he'd bought it for me from his friend, the Wyoming Valley gunsmith. I'd told Daniel's father that I had plenty of pelts to trade for a gun. He knew I needed one for hunting.

But Daniel said nothing about muskets. All he could think about was catching that Red Eye. "My father told me about a fish," he whispered. "It was fifty times your cousin's size. It swallowed a man."

"Was the man called General Washington?" I asked, wanting to make Daniel grin. He loved General Washington. Daniel said he was a great chief. He'd brave a line of musket fire. He'd risk his life for freedom.

"No fish is big enough to swallow General Washington," Daniel answered. "This man was called Jonah. He was an easy catch. Small and weak. He lived in the fish's belly for three nights. He had no water to drink or bread to eat. Jonah was certain he would die."

"Did he?"

"No. He prayed, and God, the Great Creator,

6

heard him. God said to the fish, 'Let my friend go.' And the fish spat Jonah up."

"Like Red Eye spitting gravel." Out of the corner of my eye I saw him emerge once more from the branches. The sunlight filtered through the water, lighting the gray scales on his belly.

"Coshmoo, do you believe that monsters such as a giant fish exist?" Daniel asked.

"Of course."

"Do you believe that bones can come to life and sing?"

"At night, the Ancient Warrior's bones sing and dance throughout the hills above my village. I've heard them."

My words brought the same excited grin to Daniel's face that he'd had the spring we'd found the Ancient Warrior's grave in my apple orchard. The Warrior's bones had been uprooted by a raging, rain-swollen Susquehanna. Never had we seen such long legs. Such thick arms. "The Ancient Warrior was a powerful man," Daniel now said.

"This powerful man walks in my dreams."

"I like the way you dream." Daniel's reflection smiled at me. I wondered why he spoke of dreams, giant fish, and singing bones. But I had no time to question him. In spite of our loud talk, Red Eye had come closer.

"When he gets between our hands and the shore, we'll scoop him up and fling him on the riverbank," I whispered.

7

Daniel tensed beside me. Red Eye hovered in the middle of his nest, fanning his tail.

"Now!" Daniel said.

As one, we swept our hands toward the rock. Lifted them up through the water. I felt Red Eye's weight against my palm. Shiny scales. Big red eyes. Among the sparkling drops of water, Red Eye flew. He landed at the spot where sun-baked rock met earth. He flapped into the dirt beneath the willow branches. He looked smaller than he had in water. Small . . . and frightened.

A queer feeling came over me as I grabbed him and held his flapping body in my hand. In a sudden splash of light, I saw Red Eye's world of water weeds, lurking eels, the gentle pull of current. This made me want to let him go. He didn't belong here, clutched in my hand beneath a monster sky.

Daniel touched the blue-black dot at the tip of Red Eye's gill. "We caught him! I knew we would!"

It pleased me to hear the happy note of triumph in Daniel's voice. It made me think, I can't let Red Eye go.

"Coshmoo!" a mocking voice called.

It was Flying Wolf, my Seneca cousin. He'd crossed the river behind us, where we couldn't see. His canoe nosed the willow bushes along our shore, only a few boat lengths away.

"Let's go," I said to Daniel, although I knew it was too late. Flying Wolf had seen us fishing. He'd watched us talk together in our mix of tongues and signing. Later, he would taunt me for it. I knew he would.

We sank back into the shelter of surrounding willows. The little Red Eye flapped in my hand. I glanced behind me. Through a tangle of branches I saw Flying Wolf's shadow.

"Coshmoo." Daniel pulled on my arm.

For an instant, I resisted. I knew I should stand up in pride beside a friend I'd had for more than eight winters now. But ever since I'd grown out of my cradleboard, I tried to avoid my cousin's anger. Flying Wolf was three winters older than me. Tall and strong, he liked to tease me by twisting my arm behind my back until I felt like screaming with pain.

Daniel pulled me away. We ducked through the willows and up the path that led to his cabin. The blacksmith's hammer clanged, startling a flock of pigeons. They peppered the sky above Daniel's home. Even from across the meadow, I could see the new room that was being added to it—raw, cut logs against the warm fieldstone of the chimney.

Daniel's buckled shoes and my moccasins became silent shadows darkening old and rotted leaves. Red Eye wiggled in my hand. I couldn't let him go now. Even if Daniel agreed. Flying Wolf waited for us at the river. I decided that when we were beyond my cousin's and the blacksmith's hearing, I would sing a song for the brave spirit of the little fish. The sunlight dappled him and he gasped for air, still struggling to swim free.

9

CHAPTER 2

———◆———

Daniel's cabin was built into a hill overlooking the Susquehanna. Bottles sparkled from the window that faced us as we hurried up the slope: a square-shouldered green one; another, squat and honey-colored; a clear one with a ribbed design; and five bottles colored blue like Daniel's eyes. From the time I was three winters old, these bottles spoke to me of the wonders inside Daniel's home: the scent of white man's bread, a ticking clock, and a square looking glass. Maybe, now that I was older, there would be a musket there for me as well.

"I dream of a musket. It's as loud and powerful as Flying Wolf's," I told Daniel as we headed to his home.

My friend did not pick up my hint. Instead, at the mention of my cousin's name, Daniel glanced over his shoulder. Newly budded trees embraced the sky. Everything was still and silent. Even the little Red Eye who'd been struggling in my hand.

"Flying Wolf won't come near your cabin." I wanted to ask Daniel why he was turning his back whenever I mentioned muskets, but I could wait.

"No. Flying Wolf won't. Because your mother, Queen Esther, is here." Daniel pronounced with admiration the proud name the white man had given to my mother in recognition of her power. Ever since my father had died, she'd governed my people, the Delawares. Daniel knew my mother well. When his mother had gone away to give birth to his sister, he had lived six moons with us.

The smoke from hot coals blew in our faces. It stank of burning metal. A hammer clanged. Chickens scattered as we hurried through their flock, trying to slip past the blacksmith's shed and into Daniel's cabin.

"Hold it!" Daniel's Uncle Horst called out.

We stopped. His shed was open on one side. It stood near the gray weathered barn that, like the cabin, hugged the hill. Inside the shed, hot coals burned within a stone-lined pit. With tongs, Daniel's uncle passed a knife blade over them. It was my knife, the one my mother had made me bring him to be sharpened.

"Don't go inside with those muddy shoes, Daniel. Clean them off," he said, acting as if I wasn't there.

Daniel nodded. We walked on.

"Wait!" his uncle said. "Don't let that dirty half-breed in the cabin. One in there is bad enough. Two will make the air stink."

I'd met this man three times since he'd moved here

11

in the fall. He knew I understood his tongue. I made my face like stone, not wanting him to enjoy the hurt that he caused me. The blood of many people ran through my mother's veins—Mohawk, Huron, Oneida, and white. This, along with my father's Delaware blood, ran through mine. It was proud, not dirty, blood.

Daniel's face turned red. *"Tsquallwuschink,"* he muttered to his muddy shoes.

I grinned at the name he'd called his uncle: Frog Face. It suited the ugly, thick-necked man. Frog Face stinks, too. I thought. From eating too many lice and fleas.

He put down the tongs. "What did you say?" he asked, as if he couldn't believe what he was hearing—his nephew, a white boy, speaking the Indian tongue. The muscles tightened along his hairy arms.

"Nothing. I . . . had a frog in my throat," Daniel replied, still talking to his shoes.

I felt laughter bubble inside me. Only Daniel would think of that.

His uncle's face darkened. This time, it wasn't Daniel pulling me away from Flying Wolf, but me pulling him away from his Uncle Horst. He didn't belong on Daniel's farm. He should have stayed in Connecticut, that land of the long river from which he came. The bearlike shadow he cast made me feel uneasy.

Daniel's father came out from the barn, an injured chicken nestled in his thin, pale arm. "Coshmoo," Mr. Seibert said, "I am glad to see you."

"And I am glad to see you." I spoke the words loudly in the white man's tongue. Frog Face stared at me. I stared back. He turned away and pounded his hammer against my knife blade.

"We caught a Red Eye! With our bare hands." Daniel fit himself comfortably into his father's shadow. Mr. Seibert admired our fish as he walked with us to the cabin. I felt the heat of Frog Face's angry glare.

Daniel's father opened the door. "Go on in. There's food on the table. I'll join you after I splint this wing." He smiled. The injured chicken closed its eyes. It seemed content, nestled in his arm.

"Within one night, the river will run with shad," I said, not mentioning the musket. It was his to mention first. "I hope your drying racks fill with fish."

"And I hope yours do, too. I miss having your people living across Cash Creek from me. And always at this time of year I miss your father. He showed me where to cast my nets. Eghohowin was a good friend. And a seasoned fisherman."

The mention of my father's name made something painful twist inside me. I pushed it away and slipped through the cabin door with Daniel. The ground floor felt cool and damp. One wall was formed of earth, the other three of stone. I left the little Red Eye on the wall that encircled a small spring in which two pails of milk were chilling. In my heart, I thanked his spirit for the meat. I said, It will not be wasted.

Upstairs, my mother hovered over Daniel's little sister, offering her a mug of healing white oak tea. My mother's silver cross dangled from her wampum necklace. Behind her, sunlight streamed through bottles in a window. They splashed blue, green, and honey-colored light over my mother's downturned head, and her cross and hands. My mother was no "dirty half-breed."

"Is Naomi better?" Daniel asked his mother. She fussed with the ragged edges of her stained shawl as she watched Naomi sip the tea.

"She's stopped coughing." Although his mother smiled, her light blue eyes made me feel sad. They looked dazed, as if she'd been wandering in the woods for many moons and could not find her way.

"Continue to give Naomi the tea I've brought. It will heal her." My mother spoke the white man's words with warmth. Her tawny eyes, so unlike the dark eyes of other women in my village, held sparks of gold. Never had I seen these eyes look dazed.

"I hope Naomi gets well soon," I said.

Daniel's little sister smiled shyly at me. She lifted her hands, fluttering them like a bird's wings.

"When you're well, we'll play the shadow game," I said, thinking of my father. He'd cast shadows and I'd guess what they were—a nosy fox, a chipmunk, a stalking bear. . . .

How I longed to stalk real bear. And deer. And wild turkeys, too. With a musket. I looked around the cabin, hoping to see one propped by the door. Or next to Mr. Seibert's powder kegs.

I found my mother's eyes. She shook her head. I

knew what she was saying—there was no musket—but I didn't want to believe it. I'd been waiting for a gun since last year's harvest. And then, when our trader didn't come, Daniel said his father would find me a gun. In the spring, when he went downriver to purchase lead and powder. Hollenbach's store probably had none, but Mr. Seibert knew a man who made and bought and sold fine guns.

"My father did find you a musket," Daniel told me later. He had sensed my disappointment. He sat beside me, our backs resting against the warm wood siding of his barn. On the far side, Frog Face's hammer clanged on and on. I hated the sound. "It was an old musket. But it was well made. Only . . ."

"Your father feared I wouldn't pay him for it? I've got pelts!"

"That's not it."

"He fears that even at twelve winters, I'm not strong enough to hold a white man's gun?"

"No!"

"Happy Sam would have sold me a musket. Happy Sam was planning to bring me one last fall. If he hadn't drowned, I'd be shooting deer right now!" Saying this made me feel worse. Not only for Happy Sam, our trader, whom we all had liked, but for myself. I'd used Broken Stone's musket once. I liked its loudness, the smell of burning powder, and the way it killed deer from far away.

"It's not my father's fault," Daniel said. "He

wanted to buy you a musket. But my uncle bought the last one the gunsmith had." When he saw the look on my face, he said, "Not for himself. But for the men he's gathered in case war comes here."

"War? You've said many times there will be no war! That it's only a quarrel you Americans have with your British father! That it soon will end. You said, 'Coshmoo, it won't affect your people.' But I see it does! Because it brings ugly men, like Frog Face, into our valley. Greedy men! They take all the guns!"

"I don't have a musket, either," Daniel said. "But I do have this." He reached into his pocket and brought out what looked like a bone. He rubbed it several times and handed it to me as if this yellowed bone was greater than a gun.

From the worn ridged surface, I could tell it was a portion of a giant tooth. I sensed it came from a creature larger and more powerful than any I had ever seen, for the tooth felt like the wind at the time of falling leaves—full of moonlit fields and mystery. "Where did you get this?" I whispered.

"From a trader."

"Do I know this trader? Will he come to my village? Does he have muskets?"

"No. And I don't believe he'll come here again. He . . . only stopped by."

Daniel's tone of voice told me there was more to the trader than his just stopping by. I wanted to scratch through Daniel's thoughts the way nearby chickens scratched through leaves. Maybe the trader

16

did have guns. Maybe it was Daniel's uncle again, keeping muskets from half-breeds for his *war*.

"Who is this trader?"

"He said his Indian friends call him 'Big Nose,' and he goes by that name. He wears a coonskin cap pulled down so low all you notice is his . . ." Daniel made a sign for a nose of great proportion. This made me laugh.

Daniel went on. "That tooth you hold, the one he gave me, is older than the Ancient Warrior's bones we found last spring. The tooth is older than these hills. Big Nose said it belonged to a giant water creature!"

"Like the fish that's fifty times my cousin's size?" I asked. Now I knew why Daniel had told me the story of the giant fish.

"Larger than that! This creature lived not only in the water, but on land, too. Its giant feet made pond holes. Its dragging tail formed streams." Daniel's voice dropped to a whisper. "Coshmoo, we have to find its skull. Its magic will help us stop our river from turning red with blood."

"Blood? What blood? Whose blood?"

"Our blood, Coshmoo. Your people's, and mine." Daniel stared hard at me. "The giant skull is buried in the Chemung's banks. North of your village."

"That's Iroquois country! We Delawares may be friends with the Iroquois, but no white man is allowed to travel through their land," I said, trying to digest what he was telling me. A giant skull? *Our blood?*

"I know."

"The Cayugas guard the Forbidden Path that runs along the Chemung. You must not be found anywhere near it."

"You'll be with me. You know the hidden ways. The brush piles. The mountain caves. Coshmoo, the giant skull is greater than any musket you'll ever own. My friend, listen to the story that Big Nose, the trader, told me."

CHAPTER 3

The blacksmith's tapping hammer sounded like a white man's ticking clock. It never stopped. This made me feel uneasy. Daniel touched the tooth I held, as if this portion of the giant skull could help him tell his story. "Long ago," he began, "before cabins dotted the Susquehanna's banks like fleas, a fierce war was waged on the slopes of a sacred hill just north of your village."

"Carantouan," I murmured, the water creature's tooth seeming to tremble in my hand.

"Yes." Daniel paused, searching my eyes. He knew the sorrow the mention of Carantouan might bring me. My father had died on that sacred hill. Daniel broke the small loaf of bread his mother had given him and offered half to me.

I took it, signing, "It's all right. Go on."

"An ancient tribe of Indians battled to protect Carantouan from an army of white-faced men who wore helmets. The war raged for seven times seven nights. Blood ran like a river. It stained the sky. The air stank with this blood and dying flesh. In the midst of all the slaughter, an Indian and a white-faced man fought each other over a sword. Such a sword you've never seen. Its long, curved blade could slice a man in two!

"The fighting men fell off a rampart. They rolled, over and over, both clutching the sword, until they landed in a hollow halfway down Carantouan. There they died, locked in combat with the sword between them. A black locust tree grew above their bodies. It grows there still. It has no leaves. Its bark is scarred, and its deep roots hold the two men prisoner. The black locust feeds not on earth or sunlight, but on bones."

I felt a giant spider begin dancing up my spine. It was easy to imagine a black locust feeding off bones. Black locusts are tall and gaunt. Their leaves come out late and fall off early. Their wood is hard. It burns strangely, not red or yellow, but bright blue.

"If a young warrior brave enough to face the spirits of Carantouan, and strong enough to wield the sword, were to sever the locust roots, the freed spirits of the white man and the Indian would dance happily. And all war clouds that shadow the land through which the Susquehanna flows would disappear forever."

"War clouds would disappear forever?" I said.

Daniel nodded.

"I have never heard this story."

"A Cayuga elder told it to Big Nose. This Cayuga lived within Carantouan's shadow."

"A Cayuga told this story to a white man?"

"When Big Nose was young, the Cayuga believed him to be a brave warrior who could face any spirit," Daniel said.

"The Cayuga should have faced the spirits of Carantouan himself! He should have freed the warriors!" I said. The Cayugas, whose village stood just north of mine, were one of the great Six Nations of the Iroquois. They were known to be wise and fearless.

"He tried. Many have tried. But none has ever found the black locust. It's said that only the young who dream great dreams can see it.

"Big Nose thought he could find the tree. But he became afraid and drank rum for courage. Within Carantouan's sacred territory, where water undercuts the Chemung's bank, this rum, and the pitch of the root-strewn bank, sent him stumbling into the water. He swam to shore to see a giant water creature's skull embedded in the river bank."

"The tooth!"

Daniel nodded. "Big Nose kept the tooth all this time because it came from the sacred skull. It's full of power. Big Nose, sprawled in shallow water, watched shadows dance along the skull's whitened curves. As he did, out of the corner of his eye he saw a dark-branched tree rise slowly through Carantouan's distant mist."

"The black locust?"

"Yes. Its jagged branches and the light dazzling off the Chemung made Big Nose dizzy. He fainted. When he awakened later, clouds covered Carantouan. The

21

vision of the tree was gone. He never saw the black locust again.

"Big Nose told his story to a room of men, but when I stopped to ask him about the skull, he said it was only for the young who are unafraid to dream."

Daniel looked at me. "I said I had a good friend—my closest friend—who dreams. I told him about you. He gave me the tooth and said, 'If you and this boy who dreams find the skull, its magic will lead you to the black locust. You'll free the white man and the Indian, and put an end to the fighting that plagues your valley. Then the water creature will rise on its giant bones and sing!'"

I liked the look that came into Daniel's eyes. It made me think of brave, exciting journeys. I liked the thought of singing bones. I wanted to find a giant skull, a black locust, and yet I didn't feel ready to set foot on Carantouan. I hadn't faced my vision quest, in which a boy becomes a man. I had no guardian manitou to guide me. No musket, either. I was afraid of sacred hills and their memories.

"We need to free these warring men," Daniel said. "Coshmoo, I want our people to live in peace."

Across the yard, the cabin door was opening. My mother stepped outside. The tiny bells that lined her blue cloth leggings jingled. The constant tapping of the hammer ceased.

Light glanced off my mother's hair and silver cross as she tossed bread crumbs to the chickens clucking around her. Daniel's Uncle Horst stepped into view.

Light glanced off the knife he held. My knife. The one my mother had made me bring. Daniel and I rose to hurry to her side.

She went on feeding chickens as Daniel's uncle approached. The heavy-shouldered man kept his small, dark eyes on her. As his shadow reached out, threatening a brown-feathered hen pecking near her feet, my mother turned her back on him. She picked up her basket of white oak bark.

Daniel's uncle kicked angrily at the chickens. They squawked and my mother faced him. Daniel and I placed ourselves between them.

"Your knife," the blacksmith said, handing it to me while chickens flapped around us. The part of me that hated him wanted to throw the knife away. The part that liked carving animals from wood made me touch the blade. It was well sharpened.

Neither of us spoke. I sheathed the knife while Daniel's uncle gazed at something over my left shoulder. I turned and saw smoke plume the sky. It was rising from a white man's cabin where, four winters ago, my village had stood—until men like Daniel's uncle pushed us north. Men like him always pushed my people north. From Shamokin, to the Wyoming Valley, to Sheshequin, to Tioga. I hated them.

I turned back. Daniel's uncle smirked. I felt like spitting in his frog face.

He didn't walk us to the river, but I felt the blacksmith's presence in shadows cast by rocks and trees.

23

Beneath a sycamore, Daniel's mother gave my mother red and white ribbons in return for her healing visit. I slipped the yellowed tooth to Daniel. He gave it back. "It's to remind you of a story." His voice dropped to a whisper. "Meet me. At the overlook on the round-topped hill just west of your village. The morning following the next full moon."

We pulled my canoe into an eddy created by the rock where we'd caught the little Red Eye. I thought of impossibilities: The Forbidden Path. The black locust. Carantouan. It was just a trader's story!

What if it was true? What if we really *could* stop a river from running red with blood? Smoke rose in the sky behind Daniel. The air stank of smoke and burning metal. My good friend, *my closest friend*, was watching me. I tucked the tooth into the pouch I wore around my neck.

"Coshmoo! Look!" Daniel pointed to shadows circling through the eddy. Two silver-sided shadows resting momentarily from their long fight up a river.

The shad.

CHAPTER 4

———

As I dipped my paddle through sunlit water, my mother braided into her long black hair the ribbons Mrs. Seibert had given her. The braids looked pretty next to the white wampum necklace that held my mother's cross. She fingered the cross and said to me, "Except for that uncle with the angry face, the Seiberts are good people. My heart is glad that we could help them."

"Will the white oak tea heal Naomi?" I asked.

"Her cough was in her throat, not deep in her chest. The tea should help her." My mother lifted one braid and turned it to the sun. I remember that moment always: the glow of my mother's honey-colored skin; the blue of the sky before her; and how the red and white ribbons gleamed in her fine black hair.

The seventy cabins in my village stretched out like a turkey's tail along the Susquehanna. Apple orchards, fields of corn, and pastures grazed by cattle fringed this

25

tail. Above it rose the gentle hills in which the Ancient Warrior liked to dance. At night I'd often hear his clicking bones. But when my Seneca cousins were here, the loudness of their presence silenced him.

Smoke and noise clouded the village that afternoon. On the riverbank, women mended fishnets and prepared racks for drying shad. Daniel and I weren't the only ones to have spotted them. Broken Stone, the oldest and wisest man in the village, had seen a school splashing upriver.

An excited crowd of women greeted my mother as I beached the canoe. They admired her ribbons and talked of shad. Tomorrow, rain or shine, the men and boys would have their contest. See whose canoe would net the most! But sometimes canoes came back empty. Last spring, Spotted Owl's had. Shad were fickle fish. They didn't like cold. They didn't like storms. Sometimes they swam through currents unfamiliar to the men.

"Sooner or later the shad will reach Tioga," my mother told them. "And then we will have our feast."

Nohkoomi, my mother's large gray dog, was whining. She circled the crowd of women, trying to get through them to my mother. Finally she squirmed through deerskin skirts and red and blue cloth leggings to slip her head beneath my mother's outstretched hand. I envied how well they fit together.

I whistled to Nohkoomi. I wanted her to leave these women and return to my cabin with me. I had a feeling Flying Wolf would be there. I didn't want to face him alone. Nohkoomi nosed my mother's arm, without a look in my direction.

Feeling foolish, I pretended to whistle at fluttering maple leaves and left. Gunfire startled the whistle out of me. Smoke rose from the field next to the orchard in which Daniel and I had helped my people rebury the Ancient Warrior whose bones the Susquehanna had unearthed. Three Senecas were target-shooting. They'd had no trouble finding guns or ammunition. *Their* trader hadn't died. I wondered whether they knew Daniel's trader, Big Nose. A fitful wind blew musket smoke in my face. I breathed in the acrid scent.

"Coshmoo!" a voice sang out. "Flying Wolf told me you were fishing. How many did you catch?" White Fawn sat cross-legged in front of her cabin, pounding corn in a large stone mortar. She was a slight girl, one winter older than I was. Always, we talked easily together. She hadn't become a woman yet, and I was still a boy she liked to tease. She could see my hands were empty. So could the three curious women who, with hemp, repaired a broken net in front of Bitter Weed's cabin.

"I caught many fish," I said, ignoring the women to stare at White Fawn. Her eyes were large and dark, like two pools of water.

"I don't see you carrying any fish," she said.

"I gave all my fish to Pisalatulpe, the soft-shelled turtle. He crawled up to the pile I'd caught, and whispered, 'Coshmoo. Just one? Please? I'm hungry.' Pisalatulpe, he ate them all." I held up my hands.

The gunfire ceased and White Fawn laughed. "Take me the next time you go fishing. I'll tell Pisalatulpe that he must not eat so many fish."

"I'll tell him myself," I said quickly, not wanting a girl to think that she could fish with me.

"Will you ask Pisalatulpe if he's seen any white shells on the river bottom? I'd like them for a necklace." White Fawn looked into my eyes.

My face grew hot. I wished the guns would fire again. Their smoke and noise could hide my reddened cheeks. "I'll tell him," I said, turning away so that she couldn't see.

"I know Pisalatulpe will not find any eels," she called after me. "Your cousin told me he caught them all."

"My cousin is greedy," I called back, kicking at stones. Her teasing irritated me. I was always being compared to Flying Wolf, and I hated it. "He should have left some eel for the muskrats and the river otters," I muttered. "They are hungry, too."

The three eels Flying Wolf had speared were nailed by their heads to the trunk of the sycamore growing in front of my porch. Already, he'd cleaned two. With a knife, Flying Wolf slit a circle in the transparent skin of the third. He peeled back the thin edges of skin and pulled down, hard.

I approached him warily, wishing it were my father skinning eels instead of Flying Wolf. My father had often hunted eels—he liked them fried in bear fat. My father would never have questioned my spending time with Daniel. He'd named Daniel "Chesimus," which means "Little Brother."

Flying Wolf towered over me, holding the eel skin in his hand. I felt small beneath the scrutiny of my cousin's close-set eyes. "Where is the fish you caught?" he asked.

"I gave it to Daniel," I said, knowing I couldn't tell a lie. Flying Wolf would only trap me in it. "It doesn't matter. Tomorrow there'll be shad!"

"Daniel." Flying Wolf spat the name as if it were a bitter-tasting weed.

"Daniel saw you in the log canoe. He told me he thinks you are a great hunter. He said you would return with many eel," I said, thinking this small lie might not trap, but save me.

Flying Wolf grunted. "The eel are plenty this time of year. I could have caught them in my hands." He tossed the eel skin aside. "I saw you and Daniel. You were hiding from me."

I should have challenged my cousin. I should have told him he had no right to follow me downriver. Instead I said, "We weren't hiding from you. We were playing games. You were the wolf, stalking us. We were rabbits. We tried to blend in with the willow branches, to see if we could fool you. But your eyes are keener than a wolf's."

"I am a wolf," he said. "And Daniel is a yellow-bellied dog." Flying Wolf glanced sideways at me. I saw the crazy look in his eyes. It dared me to challenge him.

Daniel was no coward. It was just that Flying Wolf was taller. At last year's Green Corn festival, he'd tried to fight with Daniel. Flying Wolf fought with his tongue stuck between his teeth. He lunged and Daniel ducked. When Daniel came back up, his head hit my cousin's chin. Never have I seen such blood.

After that, Daniel's father kept him away from Flying Wolf. Mr. Seibert didn't want two fighting boys to disrupt a happy feast. Flying Wolf twisted what had happened. He claimed Daniel started the fight, then hid behind his mother's skirts. He told everyone Daniel was a coward. Some warriors, who resented my mother's closeness with the Seiberts, agreed.

I wanted to bury this talk, and so I said, "Daniel gave me something special. It's part of a tooth. It comes from a creature larger than any you've ever seen."

"Can a tooth pay for the land Daniel's people stole?" Flying Wolf said. "I saw smoke rising from another new white man's cabin. It stands where your village used to be."

I stared at my cousin. Our mothers were sisters, yet Flying Wolf was so different from me. He was a pricking thorn! I wanted to talk of giant water creatures, and he wanted to bring up old injuries. "Daniel's family didn't push us off our land," I said. "Other white men did. Men from the Wyoming Valley."

"Behind cabin doors, Daniel's family smokes pipes with these men. They are all alike, pushing your people upriver, away from the sea. I can smell their hunger for your land. It stinks, like a hot, wet dog."

"Daniel is my friend," I said, not looking at my cousin, but at the three skinned eels he'd nailed to the sycamore. Perhaps Daniel was right. Perhaps we could get to Carantouan and free the two warriors. We had to try.

A flock of crows landed in the outspread branches of the sycamore. Their cawing announced someone's arrival. My uncle! His tall figure came striding through the trees. He brought the scent of Cayuga cooking fires with him.

Since early morning, he'd been in council with the Cayugas who lived across the river from us. But my uncle couldn't speak of the Cayugas, because Flying Wolf did all the talking—telling his father about the five white man's cabins that had sprung up along the Susquehanna since they'd visited us last fall. As Flying Wolf spoke of the wooden slats that fenced in old hunting grounds, sadness stirred inside me.

Flying Wolf paused. My uncle's eyes met mine, and then he said to me, "Coshmoo. Your hands are empty. Before you left to go downriver, you said you'd be returning with a musket."

"The gunsmiths' shops to the south of us are empty," I replied. I thought it would be unwise to mention Daniel's Uncle Horst, although I could feel him everywhere.

"A British trader came to Tioga Point today," my uncle said. His face looked stern, but I sensed a smile

31

growing inside him. "His packs are full. I told him your people had lost their trader. He said he'd heard this, and that once he's finished bartering with Cayugas, he'll come here."

"Does he have muskets?" My heartbeat quickened.

"He has five. Four of them are promised. But I've known this trader for several winters. When he crosses the river, I'll speak to him for you."

"Who is he?" I asked. Could it be Daniel's Big Nose? Traders often moved between our settlements and the white man's.

"He is a man once raised by Mohawks. He calls himself—"

"McBride." Flying Wolf said it with awe, as if the name itself held power. I felt envious of my cousin for knowing such a man. *McBride.* His coming to Tioga felt ordained. Like the coming of shad.

CHAPTER 5

That evening, the scent of frying eel made my mouth water. I liked the way my mother had prepared it—dipping each piece in cornmeal, then peppering it with spiceberries. As I waited, hungry for the taste of eel, I whittled at a chunk of seasoned pine I'd stumbled over earlier. My father had taught me how, with hand and eye, to feel for the spirit in a piece of wood and then give shape to it. I didn't know what shape this pine would take. It felt heavy, as if its spirit still was sleeping.

Overhead, stars came out. Hushed voices, talking of shad, blanketed the night. An owl hooted a love song while my uncle spoke to my mother about McBride. I listened closely. I wanted to know everything about this man. Maybe he'd become our trader and bring us supplies each spring and fall. That's what Happy Sam had done.

My uncle said McBride's muskets never exploded. Flour never laced his gunpowder, and fine trade goods always filled his packs. McBride's *friend*, the British king, was rich.

"Does McBride bring rum into villages?" my mother asked, her eyes fastened on my uncle. She hated what rum did to our people.

"He's never brought it into ours," my uncle said.

"But he will bring talk of the white man's war," Flying Wolf said, sauntering over to the cooking fire as if he owned it, the iron skillet, the eel, even the beech-nut oil in which it sizzled. "McBride hates the American settlers who rebel against the king." He kicked aside a piece of kindling to sit down between his parents. I wished I'd had a cocklebur—I would have placed it where the kindling had been.

My mother ignored him. "Our powder barrels are nearly empty and Coshmoo needs a gun," she said. "When does McBride arrive?"

"Late tomorrow." My uncle took the eel meat she now offered to him and each of us.

"In time for roasted shad." My mother's slow smile told me she'd welcome the trader. She'd feed him well. She'd fill his belly so full he wouldn't think to talk of war. I'd get my musket and then he'd leave.

"McBride loves to eat," my aunt said. "But more than that, he loves to dance! He crows as he leaps around the fire, like a bandy-legged rooster."

"He calls General Washington a cockroach." Flying Wolf glanced at me. "When McBride dances, he pretends to squash the general beneath his feet. He claims the general smokes pipes with American rebels.

McBride says General Washington plots with these rebels to steal Indian land."

This McBride could not be Daniel's Big Nose.

My uncle looked at my mother. "Your land is fertile," he told her. "Good for growing corn and wheat to feed a growing army. You must always be on guard."

She nodded and stared at the grove of trees that lined the riverbank. I felt something large and dark begin to move within me. We'd lived at Tioga for four winters now. My feet knew the hills and hollows of this land; my heart, the river's beat. Was the white man going to push us north again? Make our village, our fields, our orchard, and our hunting grounds his own? He had enough land for growing corn and wheat. His farms covered the valley south of us.

I couldn't eat. I slipped Nohkoomi the last of my eel. She rested her head on her paws and watched my knife flick bits of pine wood into the fire. I still didn't know what I was carving. A spirit was awakening in the wood: a small flutter against my palm. But it was hard to pay attention to its fragile heartbeat, for I kept seeing smoke rising from a cabin built at Sheshequin— where my village used to be. I put the wood aside.

Flying Wolf brought out a flute that he had made from bone. He rubbed it with the edge of his breechclout. While my uncle smoked his pipe, Nohkoomi drowsed, and my mother and aunt sewed moccasins by firelight. Flying Wolf began to play the flute.

The notes danced slowly with the smoke-filled

breeze. It was just like Flying Wolf to choose this sad song, whose words told of the days before the white man came. Back then, our people fished the sea. In Flying Wolf's notes I heard waves lapping, and the click of mussel, clam, and oyster shells being piled onshore. Although I wouldn't have told him, my cousin's song made me yearn for a land my father had known and loved. Until white settlers had taken it away.

Above our cooking fire, bright stars lit the night. In the distance, a rattle took up Flying Wolf's lament. A muted drum joined in as people began to sing, their plaintive voices wafting from one cooking fire to another. I thought of freshly cut timbered fences hungrily stretching northward.

That night, as I burrowed in my blanket, the notes from Flying Wolf's sad song played through my head. I fell asleep listening to them. And as I slept, a bear roamed through my dreams—a strange bear, with close-set eyes and a scar crisscrossing his broad nose, the tip of his right ear torn. The bear circled the outside of my cabin, searching for food. Hidden behind the sycamore, I watched him. Snow was falling all around me, as silent as night.

The bear discovered deer meat hanging from the drying rack. He devoured the meat, his teeth shining like winter stars. I told myself, "There's no need to worry. This bear is thin and hungry. After he fills his aching belly, he will go away."

On all fours, the bear resumed his circling.

Around and around my cabin he padded, swaying his head, sniffing the snowy night. He nosed aside the sheets of bark covering the storage pit. I shivered when I saw him unearth and eat the nuts and roots we'd stored for winter. I told myself, Now the bear has filled his belly. Now he will go away.

The bear reared. Standing on his back feet like a man, he climbed my porch steps. He nosed the latch on my door, trying to get inside.

My body was numb with cold, but my heart was hot with anger! I'd allowed the bear to fill himself on deer meat we had dried! I had let him eat our nuts and roots. This is how he would now repay me? I found myself at the foot of the steps, shouting at the bear. "You have had enough to eat! Go away!"

His eyes burned like two hot coals. They stared into mine, then dropped to the bow I was holding. A boy's bow, with a small arrow aimed at the animal's large chest. His angry roar shook me to my bones! And then, before I had the chance to fire my arrow, the dream began anew, with the bear circling my cabin. Again and yet again.

I awakened at dawn with the bear's roar ringing in my ears. My skin felt damp and cold. Fog seeped in through an open window. How I yearned for sunlight.

Flying Wolf and his father stood before our fire, drinking broth. My mother's bed was empty, as was my aunt's. They were probably outside, building fires. Preparing for shad. My belly ached.

A finger of fog swirled around my uncle, then rose

37

to touch my father's musket, which hung on the wall above our fireplace. The trigger had rusted, as had the firing piece. The musket had never worked after the warriors found it, frozen in the hard-packed snow downhill from my father's body. His right hand was clenched, defying someone. Something.

I couldn't think of this. Not now. I pulled the blanket over my head, shutting out the sight of my father's broken gun.

I heard the cabin door creak open, then hushed voices. A moment later, my uncle was pulling my blanket down. "Broken Stone just stopped by. He's ready to start the race. It's time for us to leave." I refused to look at him. My uncle's eyes were like a father's. They could read my heart. I didn't want him to see the vision that was still inside me. I needed time to think. Oh, how my belly ached.

I told my uncle I was sick. That in the night, I had burned with fever.

"You don't want to net shad with me?" he asked, "We'll catch enough to win the contest and fill this cabin. I smell fish in the air."

I wanted to fish with my uncle, and yet a bear's paw gripped me. I felt weak. I ran my hand along the rough-edged blanket, not knowing what to say.

"You waste too much time with Coshmoo." Flying Wolf stood at the door, a cross look on his face.

"Time with my nephew is well spent. One day, he will be a greater fisherman than all of us. But he is sick. I see it now." My uncle touched my shoulder. This made me want to go with him. But before I had a chance to speak, he was saying, "There is always next year's contest, Nephew. Go to sleep."

Once he left, the cabin seemed to lose all light. Braided corn and sweet grass hung from our rafters like shadows in a cave. I told myself it was a safe cave. No bear would enter here.

For a long while I lay in bed, thinking about the dream. Who was the bear? What was he? I should have killed him. Now he would always be there. Circling my home. But the next time he climbed the steps, I'd have a musket. I would aim it at the bear's large chest and fire. I was eager to see the British trader. I'd woo McBride with pelts. No one had beaver pelts like those I had. They came from a pond hidden deep within the hills. My father's pond . . .

The damp blanket chilled me. I climbed out of bed. I dipped a hollowed gourd into our copper kettle and sipped hot broth beneath my father's gun. Staring at the fire, I noticed the humped back formed by several sleeping coals. Like a scar, blackened sticks crisscrossed a graying head of ash. Above these sticks, like a large bear's burning eyes, glared two hot coals.

CHAPTER 6

———

I threw three gourds full of broth on that bear. Its red eyes sizzled, then turned black. I slammed the cabin door on the stench made by the steaming coals and raced downhill to the river. Along the fog-shrouded bank, the fires the women kindled burned like red eyes. Everywhere I turned, I thought I saw the hungry bear! Even the river noises reminded me of a large tongue lapping broth.

Frantically, I searched among beached canoes for the large one my uncle used. I didn't care what he might see within my eyes. I needed to be fishing with him. We'd catch more shad than anyone. We'd win the contest. Warriors whom I admired would pound me on the back. My mother would be pleased. I'd feel safe.

His canoe was gone. I stared at the river, trying to find him in the mist. Canoes drifted in and out of fog. I couldn't tell one from the other. Soon Gickokwita, Elder Brother Sun, would top the eastern hills. He'd burn off the mist. If only he could burn away a dream.

I raced along the bank, needing to find a canoe to share, and ducked around my mother, who was mending a drying rack with rawhide strips. I didn't want to face her. "Your uncle told me you were sick," she'd say. "So quickly, you are better? Why are you so pale?"

No one was onshore but girls and women. I stopped at fishnets spread out along the bank, uncertain what to do. The air felt heavy. Close.

White Fawn, who was carrying a load of kindling to her grandmother, Light-of-Foot, glanced at me. She whispered to her grandmother. Light-of-Foot looked my way.

I knew they talked about me, wondering why I was still onshore. I turned my back on them and searched among the fishnets for a hand net I could use. I would fish alone from rocks. I'd catch something. An eel. Maybe a Red Eye. Someone giggled behind me. White Fawn came running up to me with Laughing Water at her heels. Laughing Water was a plump girl, always happy and out of breath. Her strong-boned face emerged from the fog. It seemed to shout, "Look at me!"

"Coshmoo," White Fawn said. "We noticed you were late for the fishing contest. All the men and boys are gone."

"I'll fish by myself."

"You won't catch many with a hand net."

"Perhaps there are no fish to catch."

41

"But there are!" White Fawn twirled, grabbing at the mist. "Shad are determined fish. They always come to spawn. I feel them. They are here." She stopped abruptly and looked at me. "Coshmoo. Laughing Water and I are tired of tending fires. We want to fish from a canoe. With you."

Laughing Water giggled.

I said, "Girls don't net fish from canoes!"

"My grandmother says they can."

"Light-of-Foot would change a river's course, just to see the trouble it would cause."

White Fawn stared at me with dark eyes. "Perhaps it's time to change a river's course. Ever since my father died, my grandmother and mother and I have lived on the charity of others. We grow weary of it."

"The shad run lasts for several weeks. You can catch them later in your weirs."

"I want to catch them now. With you."

"A girl isn't strong enough to pull in river nets!"

"How do you know, until she's tried? There's more to a girl than meets your eyes. Inside, girls have the strength and fierceness of a dozen cougars. My grandmother has told me so!"

"I don't really want to fish," Laughing Water said.

"Then Coshmoo and I will go alone. Our canoe will bring back the most. You'll see." White Fawn crossed her arms. She stuck out her chin. She dared me to defy her.

"We need three people to net from a canoe." I wanted to end this conversation.

White Fawn turned to Laughing Water. "You can fish with us. You're strong.".

"My mother wouldn't allow it."

"Earlier you said she would."

"I must mind my little brother."

"Your sister can mind him."

The two of them talked on, Laughing Water finding excuses and White Fawn refusing to accept them. I searched through the woven hemp. Just as I found a hand net I could use, my friend Elk Hair stumbled through the fog and down the riverbank. Late as usual. Now as he rubbed his sleep-filled eyes, White Fawn pounced on him.

"Elk Hair!" she said. "*You* can fish with Coshmoo and me!"

I wanted my friend to dig in his feet. Stop dead and say no. But sleepy Elk Hair was like a piece of driftwood caught by the Susquehanna. Grinning, he said, "Are your arms strong enough to pull in fishnets?"

"My arms are stronger than yours," White Fawn said. "All summer, I pull weeds."

"Mine can pull a warrior's bow," Elk Hair replied.

"Mine could, too. Everyone else is gone, Elk Hair. There's no one to fish with you except Coshmoo and me."

Elk Hair looked at me and yawned. "My father and brothers are gone. And I hate fishing with a hand net. I don't care if White Fawn comes. Do you?"

What was I to say? Elk Hair was two winters older than I was. Already he'd faced his vision quest and become a man. If fishing with a girl didn't bother him, how could I let it bother me?

But it did. I was grateful for the dense fog. It hid the dip of our canoe as White Fawn stepped inside. It muffled the whisper of her deerskin skirt as she sat down. Light-of-Foot and Laughing Water would be the only ones besides Elk Hair to know that a girl was going fishing with me. I dumped the fishnet in White Fawn's lap, then climbed into the stern. Elk Hair pushed the canoe out. I winced at the loud scrape of gravel against wood, then relaxed as the silence of the swollen Susquehanna caught us.

Elk Hair paddled in the bow while I angled my blade to guide us around the sudden darkness of a fallen tree. To my left, I heard the murmur of voices, the splash of a net. We glided swiftly past. I wished I could be fishing with my uncle.

"Where should we cast our nets?" Elk Hair asked.

"Sugar Creek," I told him.

"It's too early in the season," he said.

"How about the deep channel that parallels the cattle field?"

"My father always fishes there."

We went back and forth, trying to decide where to cast our net. Finally, White Fawn said, "I know where to catch shad. It's a deep pool south of here. Near the island shaped like the back of a sleeping bear."

Her mention of bear awakened me. "What do you know about shad?"

"I know as much as you do. Shad get tired of

fighting currents. They need to rest. And that's what they're doing now. In that pool."

Elk Hair teased White Fawn, saying she made shad sound like women sleeping in the shade. But we could think of nowhere else to go. And so we let her lead us down the river.

We kept close to the bank, gliding past the sounds of dipping nets and disappointed voices coming from the deeper channels to our left. The fog swallowed Elk Hair in the bow of our canoe. It made ghosts of everything.

The island loomed out of the fog. Waves slapped against the canoe as we cut across rapids to reach the pool created by the curve of the island's paw. We paddled to a beach White Fawn said was clear of tangling brush and boulders. I knew this beach. Before Daniel's uncle arrived with his loud hammer and ugly talk, Daniel and I would canoe upstream to swim here. The island felt different now. Cold. Unfriendly.

The canoe rocked as White Fawn stepped ashore, trying to hold on to one end of the long fishnet. Elk Hair stepped out to help. The fog had lifted enough that I could see the flash of irritation that crossed White Fawn's face. She wanted to do this on her own.

"Wait here," Elk Hair told her. "Use those strong arms to anchor your end of the net."

"I know what I'm doing." White Fawn threw her long hair back and stood, feet planted apart, in the river shallows. She looked small against the angry

45

curve of pines that rose like a bristled back through the mist behind her.

I hated this island. It reminded me too much of the bear. It was easy to imagine the island's paw sweeping shad into its hungry mouth. No fish would brave such currents!

Elk Hair paddled upriver. Reluctantly, I paid out my end of the net. We circled the boundary between foaming rapids and White Fawn's quiet pool. Water pulled against the net, stretching out its webbing.

I glanced at the beach. The mist was slowly rising and I saw White Fawn lean back—a slight, dark-haired girl trying to anchor a heavy net. I hated fishing with a girl. We'd never win the contest with White Fawn. Not here. Not anywhere.

Elk Hair turned the canoe and headed for shore. The webbing, weighted down by net stones, dragged along the river bottom. I imagined the rocks and twigs the net would find. I saw White Fawn falter forward, then step back, determined not to let the webbing go.

Suddenly, for her, I wanted the fishnet to be full.

Elk Hair and I beached the canoe just downshore from White Fawn, and he took my end of the net while I went to help her. White Fawn's eyes sparkled. Her fingers curled tightly around the woven hemp.

"Coshmoo. If we catch female shad, I'll cook the roe for you and Elk Hair," she said.

I grunted, thinking, She's full of dreams.

With Elk Hair at one end, and White Fawn and me

at the other, we began to draw the long net in. All around us, the fog was lifting:

"The net feels heavy," White Fawn said, her slim arms straining next to mine.

I felt like answering, "With rocks and twigs," but I stayed silent. As we drew the webbing slowly into the shallows, one of Gickokwita's warm rays brushed my arm.

White Fawn said, "Coshmoo. Something's flapping against the net."

"It's the waves," I whispered, getting angry with her. I didn't want to deal with her hope and disappointment.

"Do waves turn silver in the dawn?" She stared at the water.

"Gickokwita clears the hills. He plays games with the mist." I refused to search the shallows. I knew what I would find.

Pulling hard against the net, White Fawn leaned against my side. I caught her musky scent. Saw the way the light hit the fine hair on her arms. Feeling uncomfortable, I looked away. It was then I saw silver bodies, saw the shallows teeming with them.

I stood still as stone, thinking, It is all a dream—White Fawn's squeals, Elk Hair's shouts, the final heave to pull the net on shore. Shad flapped everywhere, over a hundred. Maybe more. White Fawn ran from one fish to another, clubbing each quickly so that the flesh stayed sweet.

"A shell!" she cried, holding up a flat white rock

we'd netted. She tossed it into the air, and I watched it fall through the fog and tumble along the shore. In a daze, I picked it up. It *did* look like a shell, flat and fluted, ringed with pink.

"And look at this!" White Fawn shouted. She held up a dark-backed, silver-sided fish, the largest shad I'd ever seen. Now Gickokwita broke through the fog. White Fawn sang in thanks for shad, and Gickokwita poured his sunlight on the steaming Susquehanna.

CHAPTER
7

—◆—

Waves smacked the canoe's shad-filled belly as Elk Hair and I paddled it around the island's paw and into the main body of the river. Never had I caught so many fish. Their silver scales reflected Gickokwita's happy light. White Fawn, fish heaped all around her, said, "I told you I'd be good at fishing. My arms are strong!"

"Coshmoo helped you draw in the net," Elk Hair chided as we dug our paddles into the swollen current.

"Yes. But I anchored it alone." White Fawn proudly tossed her hair. "We'll win this year's contest. I just know it. Two boys and a girl! I can't wait to see the faces of the men."

I could. There'd be no end to their teasing. "Coshmoo fishes with a girl," they'd say. "Perhaps the next time we see him, he'll be wearing skirts." My cousin would be the worst.

"Girls aren't as weak and fragile as you think," White Fawn said. "Inside, they have the strength and courage of a hundred cougars."

"Last time, you said twelve," I muttered, wishing I was with my uncle.

"Last time was before I caught so many fish. See that crow?" White Fawn pointed to the bird, which, with a slow and steady wing beat, now cleared the tree tops. "I am like Crow."

Elk Hair laughed. "Crows are pesky birds. Loud and full of mischief."

"Crows are tough, and too stringy to eat. They steal needed corn," I told her.

"Crows are ugly," Elk Hair said.

"You must not know Crow's story, or else you wouldn't speak this way. Crows are wonderful birds. They do unexpected things. Listen to me." White Fawn cleared her throat and smoothed her hair back from her face. She said in her storytelling voice, "A long time ago, before the two-legged creature we call man walked Mother Earth, all the animals were happy. Gickokwita shone through the day, just as he is shining now. Brother Moon lit the night, and always, it was warm. The animals were so content they forgot to thank the Great Creator for all that He had given them. 'I must teach my creatures a lesson,' He thought. That day He turned the air so cold, Mouse had to chase his tail in circles to stay warm.

"The Great Creator made soft white feathers fall from the sky. Never had the animals felt feathers as wet and cold as these. One landed on Rabbit's nose. He sneezed. Owl laughed at him and then she named the feathers 'snow.'"

"*She?* Owl's a *she?*" I said.

"Of course! My grandmother told me this story. It must be so. Now that day, it only snowed a little. It tickled Mouse's belly as he ran in circles through it. Soon everyone was playing in this tickly snow. The Great Creator thought, 'My creatures do not listen. They still haven't thanked me. They have yet to learn their lesson.'

"He turned the air colder than before. He made white feathers fall like autumn leaves. The snow grew deeper than the tip of Mouse's tail. Deeper than the tips of Rabbit's ears. Deeper than all the small animals piled one on top of the other. Soon even the great deer had trouble walking through the deep, deep snow.

"The animals called a council. 'The Great Creator is unhappy with us,' Owl said. 'He sends cold and snow to punish our forgetfulness. One of us must go to His lodge to tell Him we are sorry and to ask for something warm as a sign of His forgiveness.'

" 'I think Raccoon should go,' said Possum.

" 'No,' squeaked Mouse. 'Raccoon's too curious. In his nosiness, he'd forget the reason why he came.'

" 'What about Owl?' Rabbit said. 'She's so wise.' "

She, I thought. Owl *can't* be a she.

" 'Owl can't go,' said Squirrel. 'Her wings are too weak for such a journey. And she doesn't see well in the daylight.'

"Rabbit thumped his hind leg for attention. 'I have it!' he said. 'We should send Fox!'

51

"Everyone laughed at this suggestion. 'Fox is too tricky,' they said. 'He'd get lost chasing clouds and swallowing the wind.'

"The animals talked and talked. The snow grew deeper and deeper. Soon it reached the treetops. And there, from the highest branch in the tallest tree, came the most beautiful voice. Even the Great Creator would stop His work to listen to its singing.

"The voice came from Crow. But not the crow that we know. This one's voice was sweeter than the chickadee's. Its feathers were colored in all shades of the rainbow.

"Crow surprised everyone by singing out, 'Let me go! My voice and beauty will charm the Great Creator.'

" 'No,' Rabbit shouted. 'The long journey will tatter feathers that delight us. Harsh winds will still a song that soothes our frightened hearts.'

" 'It's not in the nature of a rainbowed bird to take such a journey,' said Squirrel. 'You don't have the strength.'

" 'You'll crumble into a heap of sad, bedraggled feathers,' Mouse told Crow.

"As they argued, two snow-laden branches in the tallest tree broke with a crash, startling everyone. One just missed hitting Mouse. He covered his ears with his paws and squeaked, 'Oh, what are we to do?'

"Owl stared at the broken tree. Crow perched proudly among the broken branches and blinding snow, a beacon for his friends. Owl spoke: 'Crow. Beneath your rainbow feathers beats a warrior's heart.

Fly to the Great Creator's lodge. Fly swiftly and ask for His forgiveness. Our bones turn brittle and our hearts grow weak.'

"Even though his shivering friends continued to tell him he shouldn't go, Crow did. He flew for three nights. The sky felt so big, and Crow so small. But as Crow beat his wings against this darkness, Owl's words brought him courage: 'You are a warrior, brave and strong,' she had said.

"Crow winged past the stars that make up Alcor, the hunting dog. He flew bravely between the three warrior stars and the great bear that they hunt. He didn't stop to eat or drink or rest. When he finally reached the Great Creator's lodge, Crow was so happy and relieved that he sang.

"His song, sweeter than the chickadee's, pleased the Great Creator. The Creator offered Crow any gift he'd like. Crow thought of corn and fresh water. He thought of a tall pine in which he could perch. Then he thought of his friends. 'Great Creator,' Crow said, 'the animals regret that in the sunshine of their days they have forgotten to thank you for what you have given them. They thank you now, and ask for a sign of your forgiveness, something that might warm their frozen bones and hearts.'

" 'Crow. You hold a beauty in your heart that is greater than your feathers or your song. Because of this, I will give you the greatest gift of all. I will give you fire.' The Great Creator held out a stick with a large ember at one end.

"Crow felt so important—to be given the greatest

gift of all. He wanted to feel its heat and power. He was certain he could handle it. Owl had told him he was a warrior. He had just braved the fiercest night. And so, he beaked the stick a little closer to the ember than he should have.

" 'Fly swiftly, Crow,' the Great Creator said. ''I give this gift of fire but once. If it goes out, I cannot replace it.'

"Crow flew homeward, his tired wings beating even harder than before. The first night, the smoke from the stick blackened his breast and wings. He thought, 'I shouldn't have beaked it so close to the ember. But I'm the chosen one. I must go on.' The second night, the soot blackened his back and tail feathers. He thought, 'I can't drop it now. I'm almost home.' The third night, the heat scorched his beak and throat and made it hard to breathe.

"The next day, Crow brought fire to his friends. At first, they were frightened by the Great Creator's gift. Fire had ruined Crow's feathers. But fire melted snow. It warmed frozen bodies. The Great Creator had forgiven them. Rejoicing, they sang and danced around this grandfather of all fires. 'Crow! Come join us! Sing!' they cried.

"Crow was so happy for his friends. He opened his beak, and from this happiness he sang, 'Caw. Caw.'

"Poor Crow. He'd lost not only his beautiful feathers, but his voice as well. His startled friends kept dancing, pretending not to notice. But Crow was too unhappy to pretend. He fled to his favorite tree. There

54

he perched, with his head tucked sadly beneath his wing.

"At this time, the Great Creator said to Crow, 'In your pride, you made a small mistake, and you were badly burned. But pride brought you determination, too. You never dropped the stick. You saved your friends. You showed the strength and courage of a thousand cougars.' "

So this was why White Fawn thought she was like Crow. She turned and grinned at me. Ahead of her, the Susquehanna curled like a silver ribbon.

We rounded the final bend, and there was our village. Women tended cooking fires along the riverbank. Men, smoking pipes, lounged against beached canoes. Piles of shad glittered between drying racks. Laughing Water, dragging a net from her father's canoe, pointed to ours. I felt my stomach twist. *Everyone was here.*

"Coshmoo! So now you and Elk Hair fish with girls!" Flying Wolf called. He stood over a mess of fish heaped beside his canoe. I thought, He's caught more shad than anyone. This made me feel sick.

"Do you know what my grandmother told me?" White Fawn said.

"No," I answered. Why did this silly girl have to fish with me? I'd be teased forever, and we hadn't even won the contest.

"My grandmother said if we look at Crow with our eyes, we'll see only his charred feathers. But if we look at Crow with our hearts and see him standing in

55

the sun, in his feathers we'll see all the colors of the rainbow."

"White Fawn!" Red Wing shrieked. White Fawn's mother, her arms glistening with fish scales, hurried past the circle of smoking men and up to our canoe.

"We caught three nets full of shad!" White Fawn scooped an armful of fish into her skirt. She stood. While an amused Elk Hair steadied the bow of our canoe, White Fawn bravely stepped out, toward her mother's anger.

"Everyone says, 'Red Wing can't control her daughter,'" the girl's mother said. "Everyone says, 'White Fawn has become more willful than the wind.'"

"But look at the shad I caught! It will keep us through the winter!" Proudly holding her fish-filled skirt before her like a trophy, White Fawn marched past her mother, past my gaping cousin with his pile of fish, past groups of men, murmuring girls and women.

White Fawn didn't care what they were thinking. Chin up, she marched to her grandmother's cooking fire while a scolding Red Wing tailed her. Sunlight through the trees caught the toss of White Fawn's hair and turned it into rainbows. *Alla gaski lewi*, I thought—it cannot be true! White Fawn *is* like Crow.

CHAPTER
8

———

Steam rose from the shad roe White Fawn cooked in a skillet, which sat on hot coals within the firepit of her cabin. Her face flushed with gratitude when she saw Elk Hair and me standing at her door. "Come. Sit," she said. "I promised I'd cook shad eggs for you. Look. There's enough for three."

"My granddaughter caught enough shad to keep our family through the winter," Light-of-Foot, who'd brought us there, said proudly. "I will leave you to the sweet taste of the roe. But talk softly. No one must know that you are here. Imagine the fuss it would cause! 'White Fawn should never have fished with boys!' the women would shriek. 'And now you leave her to cook for them!'

"They're old buzzards—all of them! Feeding off everyone's business but their own," she said. "I'll be outside. Two knocks on the door means someone's coming, you should hide."

The door closed gently. Elk Hair and I still stood.

I believe he felt as uncomfortable as I did. I'd never been inside this cabin. It held a musky scent that reminded me of fish and dried sweet grass. Platform beds lined the walls. A pair of quilled moccasins nestled beneath white deerskin draped across the bed closest to me. I blushed, thinking, This must be where White Fawn sleeps.

"Coshmoo. Elk Hair. Sit." White Fawn's voice held a note of pleading. She watched as we sat down by her fire. "I was afraid you wouldn't come. Everyone but my grandmother seems angry with me. The women say that by handling river nets, I make men and boys uneasy." There was a sadness in her eyes that I didn't want to see. I liked how she'd acted at the riverbank. Proud and determined.

"You didn't make me feel uneasy," Elk Hair said. "You brought me luck! I've never caught so many shad."

"Not enough to win the fishing contest," she said. "And I saw Coshmoo's cousin tease him at the riverbank. Mincing after him. Pretending he was holding up a skirt."

White Fawn turned to me. "The roe I cook for you will bring the shad's fleetness to your feet. This afternoon, when Broken Stone lowers his hand to start the running race, you will leave your strutting cousin far behind."

I liked the way she said this, and hoped that she was right. Flying Wolf was fast. For the last two winters, he'd won the race to celebrate the running of the shad. But this winter, I'd been practicing. Perhaps this time I'd win.

Shad roe popped and White Fawn laughed. Fire-cast shadows danced along a wall as Elk Hair told us how he was winning last year's race, until Flying Wolf came from behind to ruin everything.

When he had finished, I said, "Last night Flying Wolf ruined my sleep. He played a song on his flute. Its sad notes lured a bear into my dreams. It was the largest bear I've ever seen."

Within White Fawn's warm cabin, with its earthen floor and woman scent, I was able to share a dream I couldn't speak of earlier. I told my friends about the bear who had eaten up the food we'd dried for winter. How he'd climbed my steps and tried to open my door. As I spoke, I relived the dream. And reliving, I now saw. "The bear's red eyes stared into mine. Suddenly, his eyes turned dark, like two black holes. In them, I felt the hunger of a thousand winters. I knew that no matter how much food I gave this bear, he would always circle my cabin. Always, he would hunger."

"How many times did you dream of this bear?" White Fawn asked.

"Many times. But all in one sleeping."

"Let me tell you about dreams," she said while carefully turning the roe to brown it on all sides. "One night, I dreamt about the husband I would have one day. He was tall and strong. Even the oaks trembled when he passed. I was proud of this husband. But as

I grew to know him, he changed. His skin grew scales. His eyes turned yellow. His arms and legs shrank until they disappeared. This husband whipped around my legs. I felt his warning rattle in my heart and bones. As he curled to strike me, I screamed myself awake. Frightened, I told Light-of-Foot, 'I dreamt of a husband who turned into a timber rattler. It was a horrible, horrible dream.'

"Light-of-Foot said, 'Granddaughter, each night for the next three nights, you must turn the soles of your moccasins upward. This will keep the bad dream away. If you don't, and the dream recurs three nights in a row, it will come true.' "

"Did you do as she told you? Did it keep the dream away?" I glanced at her moccasins. The quilled designs showed birds in flight.

"Of course," White Fawn answered. "You must turn your moccasin soles upward, too. If you don't, this bear with the hunger of a thousand winters will devour all our food and we will die."

A hot coal flared, startling me. I shivered. I didn't want to ever dream of bear again. "I'll do as you say," I said, realizing that White Fawn was unlike any girl I knew. She did unexpected things. Like fishing with boys and sharing dreams. She understood their power.

Elk Hair said, "I think this bear's been killing off our beaver."

"This bear lives only in a dream!" I almost shouted the words, for something in Elk Hair's words pricked me.

"No beaver live anymore in the ponds where I used to trap them." Elk Hair's wide, frank eyes stared into mine.

"Did you leave any to bear young?" I asked.

"Yes. But Cayugas and Mohawks have trapped the ponds as well. I've discovered their snares. They steal our beaver for pelts to buy the white man's goods— the blankets, guns, and ammunition that *we* need. It angers me to see the broken lodges. Even the dams the beaver built are giving way."

I knew of a pond that once was outtrapped, but now held beaver. My father's pond. It lay west of our usual hunting ground. I was glad I'd kept it a secret from everyone, including Elk Hair. It had been my father's wish. He loved our little brothers of the water and didn't want to see their pond outtrapped again. Each winter, he'd snare a few to barter for needed white man's goods, but that was all. This winter, I'd trapped seven beaver for pelts to buy a musket. But I'd broken no lodges. I'd left many beaver to bear young.

"If you ever dream of the bear again, you must kill it," Elk Hair told me.

"I will shoot the bear between its eyes," I said.

"And I will use its fat for frying shad roe." White Fawn offered a plate of roe to me.

The roe was hot; it burned my tongue. It tasted of fish, hickory nuts, and the lapping Susquehanna. As I ate, I asked the determined spirit of the shad to bring fleetness to my feet. I wanted to defeat my cousin at something.

The Susquehanna bordered the long, narrow meadow in which our cattle grazed. Whenever I ran through this meadow, I raced the river. I ran from the sweat lodge in the north to the painted post in the south, for this was the course we ran every spring to celebrate the running of shad. On summer days when the currents flowed slow and lazy, I was faster than the river. But at the time of budding leaves, the currents ran swift and strong. Then the Susquehanna was hard to beat.

As was Flying Wolf. Now, just before dusk, Broken Stone lined us up—sixteen boys between ten and eighteen. We jostled and joked with one another in front of the sweat lodge. White Fawn and my mother stood among the women and girls gathered at the far end of the running field. They'd cheer the first one to cross the finish line and then escort him to the shad feast. Near the women, men hovered around my uncle at the edge of the field. They placed bets on which boy they thought would win.

I wanted to run on the river side. There the Susquehanna's currents would urge me on. But Broken Stone placed me on the village side, next to Flying Wolf. I thought, Broken Stone's wisdom has told him to put two cousins who hate each other side by side. He believes this will make their legs fly faster.

Broken Stone raised his hand. I bunched my legs beneath me. Flying Wolf leaned forward. I didn't like the way this made his shadow overtake mine. I stepped sideways, to free my shadow. Down the field White

Fawn waited, small beside my mother. Ahead, and to my right, a distant splash of red moved through the stand of honey locust trees that bordered the apple orchard. I had no time to wonder about it.

Broken Stone lowered his hand. With a grateful cry, I tore off. I imagined the river racing me while a bear nipped at my heels. My legs pumped faster than a bobcat's. I passed Broken Stone's cabin and Red Wing's drying racks. I heard my cousin's heavy breathing just behind.

I ran harder, gaining speed. The tiny blossoms on the apple trees blurred into white mist; the field became a sea of green. I glanced sideways. Black Beak ran several paces behind, as did Elk Hair and Beaver. I didn't see Flying Wolf at all. I was in the lead—my feet a rapid drumbeat against the soft earth. I felt like Crow, a proud and happy warrior. I imagined myself bringing a gift of fire to the people shrieking at the finish line.

I knew this field like my own palm. My feet sensed its dips and sought out the level places. Up ahead a swell of land. I cleared it with a single leap. "Look at me!" I screamed silently, feeling a sudden watching from the trees in the curve ahead. A blur of red.

I ran on, legs pumping faster. Grass whispered to my flying feet, "Coshmoo. You *will* be the victor." I ran toward a promise of adoring looks from White Fawn. Congratulations from the men.

Pounding feet, like drums, beat the ground behind me. Closer. Closer still. I felt someone's heavy breathing hot against my neck. "Where's your skirt?" my cousin yelled, ramming his shoulder into me.

I tried to knock him with my elbow, but he was too close. He kept shouldering me. Pushing me. Shoving me hard. At the bend, his leg caught mine. I tried to stop myself, but I plunged headfirst to the ground. Before I did, I grabbed my cousin and took him with me.

Grass and gravel bit my cheek. I saw the feet of other boys running past. Angry, I tore at Flying's Wolf's shirt. We rolled over and over, kicking and hitting each other. I didn't care how much Flying Wolf hurt me as long as I hurt him. He'd tripped me. He'd made me lose a race that I'd been winning.

On top of him, I jammed my hand against his chin and forced his head against the ground. He grunted and shoved my shoulder, flipping me on my side. I heard women cheer. A gun exploded, like thunder. I saw smoke. Smelled burned powder. Someone had crossed the finish line. I relaxed my hold on Flying Wolf. He threw me on my back and sat on my stomach, his hands pinning my shoulders to the ground. Amid our heavy breathing, someone laughed.

Flying Wolf's eyes bore into mine. Spit had gathered in one corner of his mouth.

"Flying Wolf," a voice cried from the woodside. "My young friend! I greet you."

My cousin glanced where, pinned, I couldn't see. His mouth broke into a sudden grin. He gave my shoulder a parting blow, then climbed off me as if our losing the race, our anger, and our fight now had no meaning for him.

"Your arms and shoulders look strong enough to pull a warrior's bow!" a white man dressed in buckskin said in the Indian tongue. He wore a bear-claw necklace, and a red bandanna wrapped around his forehead. A long-eared mule piled high with packs stood beside him, its top lip curled.

"My legs are strong, too. If my cousin hadn't tripped me, I would have won this race," Flying Wolf said bitterly, gesturing to boys being surrounded by women at the finish line.

"McBride! Our hearts are glad to see you!" my uncle said, striding toward us to greet the man Flying Wolf said hated the American rebels and called General Washington a cockroach. A man who dealt in muskets.

McBride's nose thrust forward like an eagle's beak. Traders on both sides have such noses, I thought.

CHAPTER
9

———————

Gickokwita settled behind the hills, lighting their summits with his red-gold rays. Cattle lowed and tree frogs sang. This was the time that I loved most— the twilight between sleeping and awake. Soon I could go to bed with the soles of my moccasins turned upward. No bear would stalk my dreams. My belly was full of roasted shad, my heart full of hope. *McBride was here.*

Flying Wolf, Bitter Weed, and Spotted Owl spoke with the trader while I stood just outside their circle. I resented that I always seemed to stand outside, while my cousin, only three winters older, stood within. McBride joked with Flying Wolf, saying he'd fought off two packs of starving wolves and seven greedy American rebels to bring trade goods to Tioga Point. The trader glanced my way as he was speaking. His eyes were strange. Not green like grass or moss, but a yellow-green somewhere in between.

A rising wind ruffled McBride's thin hair, which rose above his bandanna like a scalp lock. Light from the council fire Bad Shoes was kindling gleamed off a web of angry scars that disappeared beneath the red bandanna. McBride had been badly burned. I wondered how.

Along the riverbank, girls and younger women had kindled a fire. Beside it, they sang their thanks for the coming of shad and the passing of day. Usually I'd float within the sweetness of their song, but not now. The council fire was drawing men, boys, and older women into the clearing. My mother, accompanied by Broken Stone, approached. Only she, among all women, could sit within the half-moon formed by elders. After my father had died, my people had chosen her to lead us, because of her great wisdom. Everyone grew silent as she drew near.

I sat behind my mother and Broken Stone, who counseled her on matters of war and often spoke on her behalf. I felt a little shamefaced, sitting in my mother's shadow. I'd avoided her all day, for I feared that she might scold me. She disliked any kind of fighting, especially between cousins. Elk Hair and Bad Shoes flanked me in the half-moon formed by younger men and boys. The tinkling of bells that adorned moccasins filled the twilight as older women drew in behind.

McBride nodded to my mother. He smiled briefly as his gaze crossed mine. When everyone was seated, the trader cleared his throat and began to speak. For a small man, McBride had a big voice. It carried the way a bullfrog's would, rippling the coming night.

He told us how sorry he was that Happy Sam had

died. He knew it would be hard to take his place. But he'd like to try. He hoped to be our trader now.

"My packs carry powder. Bullets. Knives. Blankets. Scissors. Beads." He spoke in the formal tone we used at council fires. "I trust you have fine pelts for me. Tomorrow we will trade. You may ask, How can McBride's packs be full of goods when most of the shops near you are empty?" He looked from one man to another, the answer dancing in his strange green eyes.

"My friends," he went on, "the British king is rich. He owns as many guns as there are grains of sand upon the lakeshore. Silver bands cover his arms from wrist to shoulder. His whisky barrels are never empty, and his women dress from head to foot in sparkling beads. When he hears that you, his Delaware children, are in need, he doesn't close his eyes and ears. He reaches into his full pockets to offer everything he has. He loves you like a father."

"If the king truly loves the Delawares, he would return the Wyoming Valley to them," Bitter Weed said. He stood next to Flying Wolf in the flickering shadows to the right of the trader. Seeing Bitter Weed's tense, muscled arm near McBride's thin one worried me. Bitter Weed was known for his prowess with a warrior's bow and for his ill temper. Even small concerns could make it flare. I didn't want him to drive the trader away.

My mother touched Broken Stone's shoulder, telling him to be on guard.

"The king does love the Delawares," McBride said

calmly. He opened the leather hunting bag strapped across his chest and withdrew a rolled piece of white man's paper. He asked Flying Wolf to hold it up so that everyone could see.

"Look at this." McBride pointed to two lines joined together in an arrowhead. "Here's Tioga Point. And here's the Susquehanna." He ran his finger along a dark line that formed one side of the arrowhead, then snaked down the paper.

I didn't think the line looked like my river. No currents ran through it. Where were the wooded hills? My village? Daniel's cabin? The shad?

McBride's hand flattened halfway down the paper. His hand moved up and down along a wide curve in the line, casting shadows on both sides. "This is the Wyoming Valley, which your great king Teedyuscung tried to save for you."

Murmurs greeted the mention of this brave king's name. My mother moaned and sadness stirred inside me. Teedyuscung had died the winter before I was born, but I'd grown up hearing of him. He had tried to establish a homeland for my people in the fertile valley south of Tioga Point.

Bitter Weed said, "The white man gave the Wyoming Valley to us. The white man helped us build fine cabins on it. Then the white man looked around and thought, This land is too good for the Delawares. Thirteen winters ago, this white man drove us out by burning the village he helped build. Women, children, and our great king Teedyuscung died in the flames."

My mother and Broken Stone conferred in whispers. I hoped they'd stop the unhappy tide of rising murmurs. McBride mustn't leave. I needed a musket.

"The king knows about this sorrow," McBride said, his voice rising above the murmurs. "See the black line that circles the Wyoming Valley? The king's war chief, Colonel Butler, drew it. He said, 'Tell the Delawares the king will do all he can to get this land back for them.'"

Astonished whispers greeted these words. Would the king attack white settlers to return the Wyoming Valley to Delawares? If the king was rich and loved the Delawares, why hadn't he done this earlier? Who was Colonel Butler?

Shadows moved and smoke rose toward the darkening sky. My mother raised her hand. Everyone grew silent, their eyes on her. "We hold great respect for the British king, who grieves our losses and wants to give back our land," she said. "And we ask ourselves, What does this great king wish for in return?"

McBride grinned. "He wants beaver pelts to make felt hats. And he asks that you remain friendly with him. Once he's subdued his unruly American children who try to war with him, the king would like you to dance at his victory feast. Already his old friends the Mohawks prepare a fire."

"As do many of the Senecas," Flying Wolf said proudly, causing several of the elders to cough in irritation. My cousin had no right to speak.

My mother said, "We have made peace with the settlers in the Wyoming Valley. Now we have a fine village at Tioga Point. We will take no side in your white man's quarrel. We build fires not for victory feasts, but for the pipe dance, the dance of friendship."

My mother looked from one man to the next. I admired the way she met Bitter Weed's frown with her steady gaze. It reminded me of how she'd stood up to Daniel's uncle. Broken Stone's eyes followed hers, affirming her stance.

McBride said, "To uphold peace is brave and noble. But keep your watch fires burning. The American rebels, unlike the British who live across the sea, always hunger for fields to plow."

"We'll keep our hatchets sharpened and our eyes on the forest." Broken Stone's eyes glowed with an inner light. My mother said this wise man could see and feel things beyond our reach.

"I will sell you war hatchets, powder, lead, and muskets too," McBride said, glancing at me. My heart leaped.

"We have pelts. We look forward to trading with you in the morning." Broken Stone turned to my mother. A slow smile crossed his dark, seamed face. "Listen to the women singing. They sound like the beaver, murmuring and sighing a love song to their young."

"It is time we join them." My mother rose to her feet.

As other men dispersed, Bitter Weed, Flying Wolf, and Spotted Owl spoke urgently to McBride. I wanted to listen to them, but my mother pulled me aside. Stars were coming out above: Alcor, the hunting dog, and the three warriors who always chase bear. These warriors carried only bows and arrows. Soon, I thought, I'll have a musket.

"My son. I've noticed how closely you watch this trader," my mother said. "Be wary of him. He opens old wounds—bringing up Teedyuscung's death." Her eyes seemed full of McBride, who, talking with Flying Wolf and Bitter Weed, now moved out of the firelight. "I don't trust this man. Look at how he walks! He leads with his nose, as if he must scent which way the wind blows before his body follows."

There's nothing wrong with this, I told myself. Our wind smells of roasted shad and hot hickory nut oil—enough to entice the nose of any man! Spotted Owl, trailing McBride, whispered Teedyuscung's name. The wind picked it up and wove the name into the warp of women's singing. The sound made me ache with sadness.

"Your father knew Teedyuscung." My mother's voice softened. "How they loved to eat peppered eel and shad together."

I stared at her. She'd never told me this. She'd told me only that Teedyuscung was a great man. He'd worn a gold-laced coat, black boots with silver buckles, and checkered pants. He'd ridden to Philadelphia to talk with the white man about Delaware land.

"How your father and Teedyuscung loved our Susquehanna!" she said, her eyes aglow. "I believe they still dance to the rhythm of our river. Sometimes, at night, I hear their footsteps on the banks. Both wanted a home for the Delawares here. A resting place for weary bones."

"It *is* a resting place for weary bones," I said. "The Ancient Warrior is buried here."

My mother smiled. "Two nights ago, while planting corn, I found bits of pottery glittering with mica. I felt the warmth of the woman who made them so long ago. My son. The presence of our ancestors reassures me. It says, 'There's no need to move your people northward anymore. This fertile land along the Susquehanna *is* your land. Indian land. It has been, for a thousand winters. It will be, for a thousand more.' "

CHAPTER 10

———

Before I went to sleep that night, I turned the soles of my moccasins upward. I wanted no bear devouring my dreams. I should have placed my moccasins under, not next to, my bed. Someone—Flying Wolf, my aunt, my uncle—knocked one over. That night, I dreamt of the bear, but it wasn't stalking me. It stalked Teedyuscung.

I watched, hidden by tall grass at the river's edge. With head bowed, Teedyuscung sat cross-legged facing me. He was dressed in a gentleman's dark coat and held a musket in his lap. Pottery was piled on one side of him; on the other side sat the Ancient Warrior, his skull white against the apple trees behind them.

I understood that Teedyuscung was there to protect our Ancient Warrior and the pottery his women made. Evening's shadows fell. One shadow, hungrier and more restless than the others, stretched across the river, darkening the shallows. It slid across the meadow in front of me and touched Teedyuscung's graying hair. Slowly, he raised his face. His eyes met

74

mine. I felt myself begin to spin like wind-blown leaves. *Teedyuscung knew me.*

He aimed his musket at the long-armed shadow that now fingered the pottery, now reached toward the Ancient Warrior's bones. Was it Flying Wolf's shadow? An American rebel's? A British soldier's? A bear's?

Teedyuscung's face whitened as he kept his gun trained on the shadow. The shadow's arm thickened and grew fur. I watched with horror as dark claws lengthened and curved. They began to scrape the long bone of the Ancient Warrior's thigh.

"Not the Ancient Warrior!" my heart screamed.

The brass hoops dangling from Teedyuscung's ears and the gold buttons on his long coat blazed. His eyes stared into mine. Said, "Help me, Coshmoo. *Help me.*"

I stepped out from the tall grass, my empty hands as white as Teedyuscung's face. I drew these hands into fists. Wishing that I had a gun, I walked toward Teedyuscung, feeling small beneath a growing shadow. A bear's sudden roar deafened me! It rooted me in the meadow halfway between Teedyuscung and the river.

As I shivered in the chilly air, it filled with the scent of burned tobacco leaves. I couldn't believe what I was feeling now—a father's warmth. I turned. Across the meadow came my father. The gleaming teeth of the shadow slashed the dark above his scalp lock. Hot panting breath breached the space between us.

Teedyuscung and the Ancient Warrior rose—tall bones whispering. They braved the bear's hot breath

75

to reach my father's side. The three strong men surrounded me.

I felt safe, so warm among them. And in this warmth, a feeling grew. It spoke of colored bottles casting light; a search for bones: *Daniel*. I felt his presence. Sensed the thorns he'd braved, the hills he'd climbed, the shadows he'd faced to be with me. He wanted to save the Ancient Warrior, too. I raised my hand and held my index and my middle finger close. Daniel slipped in beside me.

Teedyuscung held out the musket. Neither my father nor the Ancient Warrior took it, so I did, thinking proudly, *I am the chosen one. I alone will kill the bear*. But I didn't know where to fire! The shadow was growing larger. Now it darkened the apple trees' outspread branches. I glanced toward the river and saw McBride. The British trader, leaning on a silver sword, was watching me.

Outspread shadow claws raked the sky. I thrust the musket overhead, searching for the furred chest in which the bear's heart beat. Daniel, my father, Teedyuscung, and the Ancient Warrior raised their arms. Their hands locked on the musket stock above mine. *They wanted to help me*.

Chanting, we began to spin together 'round and 'round, searching the growing shadow for the bear's heart. With each turning, the musket brightened. Faster we spun. Faster still, until the musket blazed like fire. And like fire, we blazed.

The shadow roared. I never pulled a trigger, and yet I was certain the musket fired. It became a shooting star streaking through the sky. The bear retreated from its light and disappeared into darkness. We recoiled. Thrown together, we spun close—Daniel, my father, Teedyuscung, the Ancient Warrior, me.

We spun on and on, through a night that with our brightness turned into a river I knew well. The power of the Susquehanna's currents carried us past the white man's cabins at Sheshequin, through the Wyoming Valley that Teedyuscung loved, and into lands my father once had known. Finally, we reached the sea. Gentle waves caressed us. Never had I felt such peace.

I awakened in my bed at dawn. I was slick with sweat and longing. I wanted to be with my father. Know Teedyuscung. Dance with an Ancient Warrior and protect his grave. I wanted to be with Daniel, too.

I wondered if he'd awakened with such longings. Had we shared a dream? I liked the thought, but knew it couldn't be. Daniel might dream of bear and blazing muskets. He might dream about my father. He might dream about the Ancient Warrior, for Daniel loved him as much as I did. But he'd never dream of Teedyuscung.

Daniel would dream of General Washington. I imagined this Washington to be a tall man with large, clumsy feet. A thick-skinned white man whose heart could never chant or feel the rhythm of a drumbeat. And yet for Daniel, spinning with General Washington might feel the way it had with Teedyuscung. Both were powerful warriors.

CHAPTER II

I t's the best musket I have. I knew I was saving it
for someone special,'' McBride said. Fox, otter, wildcat, raccoon, and my beaver pelts—seven I had
trapped for this—were piled beside his empty packs.
Sunlight streamed through mist. Within this haze,
men carried blankets, knives, packets of powder, and
bars of lead back to their cabins, leaving me alone with
the trader and a gun. My *gun*.

"It's a Brown Bess, made by the British for boys
like you." The trader smiled as I held the musket's
wooden stock against my shoulder. I could tell that it
belonged there by the easy way the musket fit. I wondered if it would blaze the way the gun had in my
dream. I sighted down the barrel at the tree stump my
cousins had been shooting at three nights earlier. In
the mist, its bullet-riddled wood seemed far away.

"Let me show you how to aim it," McBride said.

His hands were badly scarred. By fire, I thought,
just like his forehead. He positioned my left hand on

the musket barrel. His palms and fingertips felt rough in unexpected places. His right arm reached around my back to adjust the musket's butt against my shoulder. I felt uneasy with this closeness and the strange feel of his hands.

"The Brown Bess will send your bullets to the left of the target. So you must always aim her a little to the right. Now. Hold her steady." Releasing me, McBride stepped back.

Beyond the stump stretched the meadow. Tall wind-blown grass flowed south, the way the Susquehanna did. Waves of grass seemed to whisper like women full of disbelief: "Coshmoo will never hit the target." I pulled the trigger anyway. The Brown Bess thundered against my shoulder—a great beast, full of noise and power. It sent me reeling backward.

McBride laughed. Grass and river seemed to tremble. When the smoke had cleared, we discovered a new hole in the target! It was the closest to the tree stump's heart.

I saw my mother then, a splash of blue among the watching blur of apple trees. I raised my gun in triumph. She didn't sign happiness or pride, but simply raised a hand and walked away. I told myself she didn't want to praise me in front of a trader whom she disliked.

"The Brown Bess is the one thing in this life you can depend on," McBride said. "Treat her right, and unlike people, she'll never fail you. She can kill a deer at a hundred paces."

Or a bear, I thought.

That night, I didn't turn the soles of my moccasins upward. I wanted the bear to enter my dreams. Then, with my Brown Bess, I would shoot it. To my amazement, the bear did not appear. It's good I own a musket, I thought. It had frightened the bear away. No longer would he threaten me.

If I'd known that beyond my vision this greedy bear was feeding, that with each passing season he'd be growing stronger, I wouldn't have trusted in the power of a musket. I would have turned my moccasins up every night. All winter long, I would have burned cedar needles to repel the bear and called on Meesing, the Mask Being who protects us all, to guide me. I'd have sold myself to be a white man's slave if that would have kept me from doing what I later did. The thought of it still haunts me.

McBride left two nights later. He headed north to see his Colonel Butler at Niagara while my Seneca cousins, laden with dried fish, returned to their village near the long lake of the Senecas. I was relieved to see Flying Wolf go, but reluctant to see the British trader leave. He took me target-shooting three times. He'd been patient, showing me how to load and aim and fire my gun.

"The Brown Bess will enable you to do great things," he'd said, his voice full of regret, as if he'd wanted to do great things himself but couldn't.

I looked forward to seeing him again. He promised

to return in spring. "I'll bring finely tooled hunting bags, bullet molds, and ammunition for your musket," he told me. "But I must warn you, she is a hungry beast. She eats powder and lead like a bear eats ants. You'll need many beaver pelts to keep her fed."

"By spring, I'll have a stack of pelts for you," I said, knowing a pond sheltered by steep hills. It held five lodges. Maybe fifty beaver. I'd take half. That would be enough to buy the ammunition I needed and still leave adult beaver to comb the little ones' fur. When he needed powder and lead, my father had taken at least this many beaver from the pond. And now, I had a gun.

I used more than a third of my ammunition learning how to hunt with the Brown Bess. At first I shot more tree trunks than wild geese and deer, but I grew accustomed to her ways. I was eager to show her to Daniel. When we met at the round-topped hill, maybe we could hunt before going on a quest. Maybe we'd kill a deer. We could offer its hindquarter to the water creature whose giant feet made pond holes.

Three nights before I was to meet Daniel, I shot a buck. Even Bitter Weed commented on its size and fatness. I was pleased. I hoped my mother would be, too. But that afternoon, as she butchered the deer, she seemed anxious more than pleased. I told myself it was the unusual heat. It could burn the sprouting corn.

I sat on the edge of our porch, my foot making circles in the dust while my mother's bloodied knife drew flies. Steam rose from a kettle around which three women talked as they scalded feathers off turkeys. The women admired the fine buck my mother was butchering. Nohkoomi drowsed nearby, in the shade of a sycamore.

My circling moccasin hit something tucked beneath our porch. It was the chunk of pine I'd been carving the night before the shad run. I picked it up. The pine was smooth in some places, rough in others. As I turned it over in my hands, something in the wood sang out.

With my knife, I whittled swiftly, eager to see what might emerge. Hands, I thought. A trader's hands. But what I believed to be the beginning of a finger sharpened to a beak. Now a head emerged. A cocked bird's head. A crow's. The eyes I carved held boldness, challenged everything they saw.

The heat dragged on, but I felt fresh, alive. I carved folded wings, strong young wings that could beat against the coldest night. I carved slim legs and four-toed claws, slightly wrinkled and outspread. I pared them carefully, strips of pine, like the buck's ribs, whitening the afternoon.

A breeze blew off the river, tickling the sycamore leaves. I nicked two breathing holes into the crow's bill as White Fawn walked by. She was carrying river water to the women's fire. She paused to pet Nohkoomi.

"What are you carving?" she asked.

I handed her the crow. I felt anxious as she turned

it over in her hands. She'd told me Crow's story. Her spirit was tied up with crows. I hoped that she would like this one.

"You will dye it?" Her hand caressed the crow's head.

"With black walnut juice."

"It's a beautiful crow. Only . . ."

"Only what?" My heartbeat quickened.

"Something's wrong with his eyes. When I look at them, I feel as if I'm seeing the crow, but not hearing his true song."

I studied the crow in White Fawn's hands. I tried to understand what she was saying. "What do you know about real crows!" I told her, taking it away. "This crow is a warrior." I decided I would give the crow to Daniel—after we'd found the dead black locust tree. The crow's bold song would bring us courage to free the fighting men.

My mother arose early two dawns later when I left to meet Daniel. The crow, blackened now with walnut juice and wrapped in leaves, nestled against the musket balls I kept in my deerskin pouch. Mourning doves were cooing. My mother stirred pottage in a big iron kettle, her tense movements at odds with the slow and easy morning. "You are going hunting?" she asked.

"For squirrels, raccoons, maybe another deer. An easy hunt. I'll be back by sunset," I replied.

"You hunt alone?"

"Yes." I hated the lie even as I said it. But my

mentioning Daniel would lead to more questions and then more lies. Daniel and I planned to hunt for giant bones in Iroquois country. We might trespass on a sacred hill that held fighting men and memories. I could never tell my mother this.

"Sunrise to sunset is too long a time to hunt on an empty stomach." She filled a small deerskin pouch with *tassamane*, the dried cornmeal that a hunter carries on long journeys. She handed it to me. Her eyes looked tired and sad.

"What troubles you?" I said.

"It was hot last night," she answered. "Mosquitoes whined around my head. They made it hard to sleep."

"We'll burn cedar needles on our fire. The smoke repels mosquitoes."

"Will it repel uneasy spirits?" she asked.

I glanced at her, then turned away, afraid of the intense look in her eyes. The sky was growing light.

"My son. Even the spider weaves his web so that his home faces south." She began to scrape the edge of a wooden spoon around the inside of the kettle. I wished she wouldn't do this. The sound reminded me of a long-ago time. A distant sadness—my father.

She continued scraping. "He who was your father has been in Assowajame for many winters. He should be there now, like a contented spider basking in the sun. But ever since that moment McBride taught you to fire a gun, I've sensed your father's presence. It feels like the low rumbling from a far-off storm."

"Why is my father troubled?" I wanted a reason, yet was afraid to hear it. Deep inside, I knew.

"I am uncertain," she said. "The past three nights, I've seen his spirit. It comes from nothing, to appear suddenly, a green glowing ball. It hovers over our mantelpiece, lighting up—"

"His musket?" I asked.

My mother whispered, "Yes."

CHAPTER 12

———

The night before my father died, he'd tried to teach me how to split and carve seasoned ash to make a bow. His trembling hands fit my forearm against the stave to measure length. I remember how my fingertips curved around the end. Steam from the white oak tea my mother brewed warmed our chilly cabin.

Wrapped in a thick red blanket, my patient father watched as I scraped and carved. I listened to his every word, but my small hands were clumsy. They would do nothing that I wished. Finally, I threw the bow aside. I stood up, wanting to leave the steamy cabin and my father's questioning look. "The wood's no good!" I cried.

"You must take time to feel the ash and listen. This wood sings a hunter's song," he said.

"Making bows takes too much time! Our men have muskets for hunting!"

"My son. The musket . . ." He covered his mouth and coughed. I waited, a boy eight winters old who was impatient for his father to finish speaking. I didn't want to make bows. I wanted to go outside. Make footprints in the newly fallen snow. Skate my moccasins along a frozen stream. I didn't know how sick my father was. For many moons, the cough had been a part of him.

My mother gave him tea, and then he spoke. I remember that his voice reminded me of water rushing over stones. "The musket sings a strange song only the white man understands. We don't know how to make this musket or mend a broken one. As for ammunition, we must depend on traders. And if the powder is damp, the musket won't fire.

"But bows and arrows come from trees rooted in our land," he said. "We understand their song. As long as branches embrace the sky, we can fashion bows and arrows. And even if this sky rains hard, we can hunt."

"But *you* hunt with a musket! I want to hunt with one, too," I said.

"I'm a man, grown old and tired. You are young. Your arms are strong enough to use a bow."

My father's hands fussed with the blanket drawn around his shoulders. His hair was turning gray, but as long as I could remember, he'd hunted with a gun. He'd killed geese, turkey, bear, deer.

"*You* hunt with a musket!" I repeated. "*You* haven't used a bow for many winters!"

"I'm too old to be a father!" he blurted out, his eyes glistening with tears. "And I am weak. I depend

87

too much on the white man's ways. My son. Do not be like me." His voice softened on these last words. He closed his eyes, hiding the tears I hated to see.

He went to bed. And as he dozed, my mother spoke. Her voice whispered like the stirrings of her wooden spoon against the kettle. "Your father is a wise man. The old ways are often best. But his eyes grow dim, or else he'd see. Our arrows are no match for musket balls. In this land hunted by both Indian and white man, we must have guns. We need them to survive."

I had glanced at his musket then. It hung, dark and silent, above the fireplace. I stared at the carved stave I'd thrown aside. Strangely, this wood, unlike the musket, seemed to come alive. It grew before my eyes. I saw a trunk rise clean and simply, touching sky. I heard the wind sing through ash leaves. I saw long-limbed warriors drawing bows. This vision spoke to me.

Through the evening, as my father slept, I worked hard to make a warrior's bow that would bring him happiness and cause him to say, "My son makes me proud!" I fell asleep with these words in my head. When I awakened in the morning, my father was gone. I didn't see him again until our warriors brought him home. They'd followed the tracks his bare feet had made through snow, and found his frozen body sprawled next to a rampart on Carantouan, the sacred hill. My father wore nothing but a breechclout.

His right hand was clenched in a fist, as if he were

defying something. The wind spirits that gathered at Carantouan's summit? A frightening vision he had seen? His dependence on the white man's ways? Our warriors found my father's musket downhill from his body. The gun had been smashed against a tree.

I didn't sleep well for many nights. Neither did my mother. "It was not our talk of muskets that drove your father to Carantouan," she'd croon, rocking me. "A raging fever did. It made him think that knee-deep snow was sun-warmed grass, and ice-coated Carantouan, a summer hill filled with sweet-smelling dreams. Why else would he go there barefoot, with no bear-skin robe or blanket?"

She said nothing about the smashed gun or my father's fist. His eyes, frozen open, had held such sorrow! Blood caked his mouth and chin the afternoon our warriors brought him home. My mother cradled his head to her chest. I remember his gray hair against her black, his tan skin against her red wool shawl.

My mother hung my father's musket back above our mantelpiece. We didn't speak of his death again. I buried the memory of his dying the way a mountain lion buries prey. I grew out of pain into wanting a musket of my own. I needed one.

"I won't give up my musket! I can't!" I told my mother now.

She stirred the pottage, its bubbling the only sound in the strange chill of the morning. A bird's shadow winged across the kettle. She reached out, as if she thought that she could grab it. Opening her hand, she smiled gently at the motes of sunlight she'd caught. "Your father told me you saw things in shadows that were beyond his knowing. His hope was that you, a dreamer of dreams, would create a homeland for his people."

"I *will*. With this!" I held up my musket.

"Go, then. Hunt. Kill me another deer," my mother said. "I will throw its fat upon the fire to feed your father's spirit. I will place kettles of food upon his grave. I will tell him that with a son like Coshmoo, he has no need to worry about anything, including guns."

As I climbed the rocky path that led to Daniel, I thought of how my father had measured my forearm to make a bow. To make a musket, he'd need to measure me from the shoulders down. He'd need iron. And brass. And walnut for its stock. He'd need to know the magic of a firing piece. How to carve a trigger.

I dug my moccasins into the path that spiraled the round-topped hill's grizzled face, and cradled my Brown Bess. She felt a part of me. I fingered the deadly curve of trigger. All I had to do was pull it. Her answering bark would make the valleys tremble!

I saw Daniel before he saw me. He stood on a large gray boulder that overlooked the valley, the blue of sky behind him. He wore a fringed hunting shirt and leggings, and a round hat I'd never seen him wear before; a buck's tail stuck out from the brim. Daniel cradled a musket, too.

Seeing me, he thrust his musket in the air. "Cosh-moo!"

I liked the way he called my name. It echoed through the hills. I liked the way he held his gun aimed at the sky.

I scrambled up the rock to greet this friend who'd traveled far to see me. He grinned. "An omen. A good one," he said, pointing to his gun, then mine.

CHAPTER
13

———◆———

Daniel and I stood together on Round Top's high expanse of rock. The muddy Chemung ribboned the valley below us. In the distance, the Susquehanna curled to the east. Carantouan stood sentinel between these rivers. Pointing to the sacred hill, Daniel said, "Our journey will end there."

He shouldered his new musket. It was longer than mine and had an iron ramrod instead of a wooden one. As we scrambled down the rock to begin our journey, I told my friend, "Carantouan holds sad memories for me."

"I know," he said. "I remember the day warriors brought your father's body home. But Coshmoo, we *must* go there.

"Did you bring the water creature's tooth?"

I handed it to him, and Daniel's eyes grew soft with dreams. "Big Nose said that all bones are connected: the water creature's, the Ancient Warrior's . . . the bones held captive on Carantouan."

"Your bones and mine."

He grinned as he returned the tooth. Ahead of us, smoke snaked through the treetops. "Cayuga watch fires," I whispered. "We must be wary of Cayugas. They guard the entrance to the Forbidden Path. If they found you near it—"

"They'd think I was spying on them. The Cayugas would skin me. Especially now."

I stared at my friend. "What do you mean?"

"Seven nights ago, three Cayugas came downriver to our farm. My father was sick in bed. My uncle ran them off."

"But why? As long as you don't trespass on Iroquois territory, the Cayugas won't harm you."

"Someone torched a settler cabin near ours. One neighbor, Mr. Jenkins, claims Cayugas did it. Another says it was Tories dressed as Cayugas. My uncle chooses to believe Mr. Jenkins. Because my uncle hates all Indians."

Daniel kicked angrily at stones. "The Cayugas who came to our farm only wanted him to sharpen their knives! My uncle said, 'Why should I? You'll use them to carve our throats.'

"I was pumping bellows, blowing air on my uncle's coals. I wanted to turn the bellows on his face. I wanted to blow my uncle away. These Cayugas had come peacefully."

"Was one of the Cayugas an old man with long gray hair?" I asked, picturing Kschilaan, the Cayuga sachem. He was a proud man, known for his wisdom and great courage. If he were insulted . . .

"The three men were young," Daniel said. "The

tallest had torn earlobes with feathers and beads attached to them. This Torn Earlobes said, 'The British blacksmiths can sharpen knives as well as any American. We will go to them.'

" 'Bloody Cayugas!' my uncle cried. He fired his gun above their heads. The three Cayugas didn't flinch. Torn Earlobes flipped his knife blade back and forth against his hand. When the musket smoke had cleared, he and the other two turned their backs on Uncle Horst and walked away.

"Now my uncle imagines Cayugas with sharpened knives hiding in our haystacks, in our woodpiles, even in our barn. He's formed a militia with other men from the valley. He says it's to protect our land from the British, their Tory allies, the Cayugas, and their friends across the Susquehanna . . . the Delawares."

Daniel stared at the ground as he was saying this. We walked side by side down the worn path that snaked along the west side of the hill. I clenched the water creature's tooth in my chilled hand. I said, "Your people and mine share the same soil. We give each other medicine to heal our sick. We will never go to war."

"My father believes that, but my uncle says, 'The Delawares killed settlers during the war between the French and British. What's to keep them from killing settlers now?' "

"Their friendship with them." I watched a chipmunk dart across our path. The darkness between two boulders devoured the animal's small striped back. This and something else bothered me. For a short time, Teedyuscung had joined the French in their fight against the British. As war hatchets were being buried, white settlers had killed him.

"My uncle says the British king plans to court the Indian tribes who live near Tioga. He'll buy their allegiance with trade goods. Then he'll position troops at Tioga Point."

"No British king will buy our allegiance! No troops will kindle fires at Tioga! It's been Indian land for a thousand winters!" I said.

"The king wants to control the northern gateway to the Susquehanna. Because it flows from the country of the king's friends, the Iroquois, southward through the Wyoming Valley to the sea."

The sea. Once my people had fished the sea. Until white settlers pushed us north. Would the British king push us even further north? But no. My people would never let that happen. A breath of hot air blew in my face. It smelled rank, like bear.

"It's good we're going to Carantouan," I said. "Tell me your trader's story again. I want to hear about a giant skull with large, sad eyes. And a dead black locust tree that rises out of mist. I want to know how two boys like us can free fighting men forever."

We'd reached the bottom of the hill. As Daniel led me west, following a dry-bottomed creek, I got caught up in the war between the Indian and the white man that raged seven times seven nights. I saw the blood that painted the sky. I smelled the heat of a flaming sword. I heard men's dying screams.

Daniel led me from one large stone to another as he

now spoke of the water creature buried in the bank of the Chemung. His voice and the tooth clenched in my hand seemed to sing together, about feet larger than copper kettles. A skull, five times larger than these feet. An eye. "The sight of the bones will make us feel like this," Daniel said, running his finger up my spine.

"But will the bones lead us to the locust tree?"

"Yes."

A part of me felt like saying, "This trader's tale is too big to believe. Let's visit the Ancient Warrior's grave. Let's sit beneath the apple trees and make whistles out of grass." But another part wanted to explore the bank of the Chemung, climb a sacred hill, cut away dead roots. I wanted peace to rain on our valley. I loved its rivers, its meadows, and its hills. I wanted to live always as I was living now: hiking with a friend, searching for giant bones with him, hopping from one stone to the next.

CHAPTER 14

———

Daniel and I kept watch for Cayugas as we veered off from the dry creekbed to wade down a stream Big Nose had said was formed by a water creature's dragging tail. The stream, meandering northward through deep woods, gave wide berth to the Cayuga watch town across the river from my village. I saw no bent twigs, painted trees, or moccasin tracks. Wind played with the buck's tail in Daniel's hat and made it dance.

I said, "I like your hat. It makes you look important."

"I call it my George Washington hat." Daniel pulled the brim down until it covered his eyebrows. "My father got it for me."

The proud way he said "father" reminded me of mine.

The winding stream led us a little north of Carantouan and then doubled back. We were north of the Cayuga watch town now. North even of Carantouan.

The land was full of unexpected pond holes Daniel said were made by giant feet. Marsh grass ringed these holes. Turtles sunned themselves on logs. A flock of geese paddled lazily across one pond.

I aimed my musket at a fat gray goose that preened, then went bottoms-up searching for something good to eat.

"Don't fire," Daniel said. "You'll alert Cayugas."

I laughed. "I wouldn't waste my ammunition on that old goose."

Daniel grinned and held up his gun. "Look at this—a bona fide American musket made in Pennsylvania."

I held mine up beside his. "Mine's a Brown Bess. McBride said the British made it for boys like me."

"Who's McBride?"

"A trader."

"A British trader," Daniel guessed, checking my face for affirmation. "But the British cheat. They lie. They're traitors to the cause of freedom. You mustn't deal with them."

"McBride doesn't cheat or lie. And he has muskets, blankets, knives, and ammunition for us. What does it matter if he sides with the British or Americans?"

Daniel said it did matter. The British king charged three times what his goods should bring. Worse than that, his traders were spies. They traded with Indians only to ferret out news about American settlers to take to the king.

Daniel's voice lowered as if the stones and leaves had ears. "The woods are full of spies. You never know where they might be hiding. Last spring, in the fighting at Lexington, a British trader, claiming to work in secret for the Americans, befriended an American lieutenant.

"The trader told the lieutenant of a cabin in which three British spies planned to meet. The trader said a small battalion could easily overtake these men. They'd be a prize catch.

"When the lieutenant and his five men approached the cabin, twenty British soldiers and four Shawnee scouts surrounded them. The British trader had betrayed his friend."

Daniel couldn't recall the trader's name, only that it sounded hollow, like an echo in a cave. Daniel said he carried silver-mounted pistols that gleamed like sunlight off the stream. His skin was pitted like the ash tree's bark; his eyes, two stones. It was easy to imagine this trader in all that was around me. He sounded a little like McBride.

Ahead of us, the forest lightened. In the distance, we could see Carantouan rising above the trees. We were entering sacred territory. I felt my skin grow clammy.

"The trader watched an officer question the lieutenant about the movement of American militia," Daniel continued. "When the lieutenant refused to answer, the trader stood, arms crossed, as British soldiers and Shawnee scouts tortured his *friend*. He listened to the lieutenant's screams as they stuck flaming splinters into his skin. The lieutenant cried out to the trader, 'End this agony. Shoot me. Please.'

"The trader laughed. He gave his gun in its holster to a Shawnee. He held his hands up and said, 'I can't shoot. See? I have no gun.' "

We'd reached the Chemung. At our feet, the small stream flowed into the river. I crouched. I dipped my clammy hands into the cool, dark water.

"The lieutenant shouldn't have cried out," I said. "If he had shown courage, the Shawnees might have saved him. And even if they didn't, he would have died with honor."

"Would you just stand by and watch me die? With or without honor?" Daniel's eyes searched the tree-lined bank for bones.

"If my people took you prisoner and condemned you to die, I would stand beside you. My heart would beat with yours and you wouldn't be afraid. You would face death like the bravest warrior," I said, never thinking this might happen. Or that words, like courage, could be tested.

Daniel glanced at my reflection in the water, then stood. "I couldn't watch you die. I'd attack your enemies. I'd shoot them in the belly."

"And if I was a spy and my enemies were your people?" I asked, looking up at him.

"It wouldn't matter. I'd do anything to free you." He studied the Chemung. It ran low for this time of year, too low. The spirit of a water creature whose dragging tail formed streams must have opened its large mouth. It must have taken great swallows of the Chemung to expose its banks.

"Don't deal with the British," Daniel said. "They'll hurt you. They'll betray you."

"Who told you about the trader whose name sounds like an echo?" I asked, unwilling to give up McBride. He'd brought me a musket. He'd promised to bring lead and powder next spring.

"Uncle Horst."

An image of a large, hulking, dark-furred man flashed through my mind. Daniel's uncle would spread tales about anyone. Because he hated everyone. The British. The Cayugas. The Delawares. Me.

"Coshmoo!" Daniel whispered. I stared where he was staring. A willow's roots clung to the Chemung's bank. I lost my breath when I saw what these roots held—*a skull*.

Only portions could be seen. Yellowed bone encased a dark clay eye. This large eye peered at us from between two roots. It was the eye Big Nose had seen.

Three teeth rose from what must have been the water creature's lower jaw. A whitened tusk curved and disappeared into the bank. Beneath the tusk stretched a bone as big around as a warrior's thigh. I sensed the power of the creature's presence ten paces away.

I wished I'd faced my vision quest and been blessed with a manitou. This guardian spirit, my link with the world beyond, would tell me how I should approach such bones.

"It's just as Big Nose said." Daniel knelt on the

muddy shore. He began to pry rocks and soil away from the skull.

"No." I pulled his hand away.

"I want to free it."

"These bones are a part of Mother Earth. They belong to her. It's the fighting warriors we must free." As I said this, I felt a chill. A darkness. I turned slowly, expecting to see a black locust tree rising through mist. But the chill was a gust of wind. The darkness, cloud shadows racing across a distant summit.

Daniel said, "Big Nose studied the skull before the locust tree appeared. We must do the same."

I brought out our piece of a giant tooth and, kneeling beside Daniel, replaced it in the water creature's jaw. The Chemung lapped at the toes of my moccasins. Mud seeped through my leggings. Dappled sunlight played off the bones.

I drifted with shadows dancing down a curve of tusk and began to feel a little strange. The more I drifted, the stranger I felt. Suddenly, I found myself outside myself. I was a giant skull, looking at Daniel. Carantouan, the sacred hill of dreams and visions, seemed to tower behind my friend, and I asked Daniel something I'd never asked him. "My friend. Why does your uncle hate me?"

"I told you. He hates all Indians."

"But *why*?"

"I don't think that I should tell you."

"Tell me anyway. I must know."

Daniel's eyes gazed into mine, bringing my spirit back into my body. He said, thirteen winters ago, his uncle had a sturdy cabin south of Sheshequin in the fertile Wyoming Valley. It sheltered him, his wife, and three small sons—Aaron, John, and Conrad. "One morning, Uncle Horst left this happy family to go hunting," Daniel said. "When he returned, they all were dead. Even the dog. Delawares murdered them. They claimed it was revenge for a great king's dying."

"King Teedyuscung," I whispered.

"You knew him?"

"My father did. Teedyuscung was making a homeland for my people in the valley your uncle found so fertile. The white man set fire to Teedyuscung's cabin. The flames killed him and drove my people out. Such a death calls for revenge."

Daniel said softly, "The Delawares killed my aunt. They killed my three small cousins."

"The white man's flames burned many cabins. Some held Delaware women and children," I said, feeling uncomfortable on this shore. It was time to search for the black locust tree. I could feel it near.

But Daniel wasn't ready to leave. He ran his hand along a whitened tusk and said, "Once this was a great and powerful creature. It must have ruled the country east and west, and north and south of the Chemung. Perhaps it even ruled the skies above. And now it's only bones. Touch them, Coshmoo."

When I hesitated, Daniel took my hand in his. He ran our hands along a cool, dry stretch of tusk.

"Why do you think a creature as great as this one died?" I asked.

"I think the valleys of the Chemung and the Susquehanna were not big enough to feed it," Daniel answered. He ran our hands along the smooth curve of the skull, traced the worn surfaces of teeth that might have torn giant reeds out of mud and stone, followed the outline of an eye that probably had seen creatures far beyond our knowing.

The skull warmed to our touch. The water creature was about to speak. It would open our eyes to the dead black locust. Two boys, not afraid to dream. We would free the fighting Indian and white man! I glanced to my left, hoping to see the tree.

I should have known that there would be briers. That a quest like this would not be easy. Then I would have been alert. My eyes would have sensed approaching shadows; my ears, the dip of paddles; my nose, the Cayugas' scent.

CHAPTER 15

———

The Thunder Beings are large birds with human heads. They live in the sky and feed on soup made from old, dried bones. They carry bows and arrows with which they send bright bolts of lightning through the sky. Sometimes these arrows shatter trees and cabins.

One of their arrows split the sycamore the day after my mother and Broken Stone had escorted me, shamefaced, home from the Cayuga village. The tree cracked just above the spot where, earlier, Flying Wolf had nailed eels. The lightning didn't destroy the tree, but weakened it. The following spring, leaves sprouted from the lower limbs, but the upper limbs were dead.

The day the sycamore was struck, Nohkoomi cowered beneath my mother's bed. Rain lashed against our skin-paned windows. Arrows lit the dark outside. Inside, I painted plum pits to make dice while my mother, in unusual anger, railed at me. "You shouldn't have taken Daniel onto Iroquois land. Look at the trouble you've caused. We are a small village. It would be easy for Cayugas to call on Iroquois forces. Easy to destroy us. And when Elk Hair tells Daniel's uncle that he must travel to Kschilaan's village to barter for his nephew's freedom, his anger will cause the ground to tremble."

"But Daniel's father should do the bartering— everyone likes and respects him. Not his uncle!"

"His father is too frail to make the journey."

"The Cayugas will free Daniel anyway. They must." I needed to believe this above all things. I couldn't forget the way Daniel looked when I'd left, standing small beside a tall Cayuga with torn earlobes who wore Daniel's hat. I knew what this hat meant to Daniel. I wanted to say, "It doesn't matter. The spirit of your General Washington doesn't live in a hat." But by then, a stern-faced Broken Stone had seated me in his canoe.

"I spoke for Daniel," my mother said. Her voice softened. "Kschilaan knows his father. The Cayuga sachem says the farmer's an honest man, but the boy's uncle is a powder keg—ready to explode. Kschilaan suspects that this hate-filled uncle sent Daniel to spy on the Cayugas."

"He wasn't spying! Daniel wanted to find the black locust tree and free the fighting men. He wanted to save the Susquehanna—"

"From turning red with blood. I know. You've told me this story three times. And each time I ask myself, 'Is my son so foolish as to believe a white man's dream?' "

"You believe a white man's dream." I stared at my mother's cross. It glittered with firelight as she stirred pottage. I imagined the sad-faced man who'd hung on such a cross. Did he sense my pain?

I continued painting my plum pits while questions stormed inside me. What had happened to Daniel? Where was he now? Did Cayugas question him? I glanced at the wooden crow I'd stuck on the storage shelf above my bed. I wished I'd had the chance to give it to Daniel. The crow's bold eyes would bring him courage.

"If my son believed a white man's dream, why did he fear sharing it with Kschilaan?" my mother asked her sputtering pottage. "Even the two red blankets and the fine brass ladle Broken Stone and I offered for Coshmoo's return didn't wipe the questions from the Cayuga sachem's eyes. Why did this boy lie to him— saying a deer they'd wounded had led them deep into Iroquois country? Bah! Neither musket had been fired! Why had this Delaware boy brought a white farmer's son onto forbidden land?"

I resented the way that she said *boy*. A *boy* did foolish things. A *boy* got lost in dreams he was afraid to share with sachems. But I feared Kschilaan would have taken away my musket, my powder horn, my hunting bag—he might have stripped me of everything if he had known I'd planned to take Daniel onto Carantouan.

I recalled how my moccasins had stood defiantly next to Daniel's buckled shoes so that our legs could shield the water creature's bones from the Cayugas' eyes. Instinctively, we had done this. Even though we were in Iroquois country, we'd felt that these wondrous bones were ours. We had found them. Nothing, not a mother's anger, Kschilaan's suspicions, or a frog-faced uncle, could ever take that fact away.

"Rumors spread like flies," she went on, talking to her pottage. "Some think Queen Esther's son has become a white man's spy."

"I'm no spy! I'd never betray my people. Or betray a friend," I added, thinking of the British trader's silver pistols and his treachery.

"Whispers of a coming white man's war gather like the mists around Carantouan. Kschilaan fears the fighting that began in the north may soon come here. He says both American rebels and British sympathizers live along our river. Like snakes, they hide among the rocks and bushes. They listen to the Cayuga heart, and ask, 'For which side does it beat?'"

"Daniel and I don't care about Cayuga heartbeats! We only want to save our valley from war. Is it wrong to follow dreams?"

"Dreams." My mother, who had always believed in dreams, spat at the fire. "It's too easy to get lost in them! A cougar crouches in an oak tree. Do we see it? No! Because we're watching the way the oak leaves dance."

"Daniel's uncle is the cougar," I told her. "He runs friendly Cayugas off Daniel's farm. He forms a militia.

Not only to fight off the British, but to fight our people, too. He hates the Delawares. He claims we killed his wife and sons in revenge for Teedyuscung's death."

My mother's face paled. "I don't want this wound reopened. We've lived in peace with the white man for thirteen winters, both here and at Sheshequin. We have a fine village now. Seventy cabins. Pastures of cattle. Apple orchards. Nothing must destroy this."

"But the old wound already bleeds," I said. "Daniel spoke of Teedyuscung. McBride and Bitter Weed did, too. And now, I dream of him. He sits in our orchard."

"Do not tell me this."

"Teedyuscung is dressed in a gentleman's dark coat," I went on. "With his musket he guards the Ancient Warrior's bones. Evening falls, and a shadow reaches out to finger Teedyuscung's hair."

It was the first time I had shared this dream with anyone, and the telling of it raised the small hairs on my arms. "I hate this shadow!" I told my mother. "I run to Teedyuscung, wanting to help him fight it. As I do, the shadow thickens and grows fur. Claws lengthen and curve. They begin to scrape the long bone of the Ancient Warrior's thigh."

"The bear." My mother's gasped words startled me as much as the thunder that crashed outside. A jagged flash speared the night. Our cabin trembled and filled with an acrid scent. Outside, the sycamore's upper limbs were dying.

My mother threw tobacco on the fire, asking that

its smoke appease uneasy spirits. The Thunder Beings rumbled. As rain warred against our cabin walls, my mother told a story. It spoke of a great chief who wore a white-man's coat with twenty-six brass buttons. He loved this coat, for when he wore it, white men flocked to entertain him. But in his nightly dreams, the twenty-six brass buttons turned into a great bear's sharp, gleaming teeth.

My mother said, "Teedyuscung told your father that he didn't know what to do. 'I can't give up my coat. But the bear's teeth devour everything—trees, corn, shad, pigeons, beaver, land. I try to fight it, but it's more elusive than the wind.'

"It was six moons after Teedyuscung's death that your father told me this. Captain Bull, Teedyuscung's son, had just returned. As your father spoke of coats and bear, Captain Bull's cries of revenge for Teedyuscung's death rustled the maple leaves patterning the sky above our village. I remember these leaves, for they were colored red. Like blood."

She paused. Rain slammed against our bark-shingled roof. Firelight flickered, casting shadows along the walls. I paced, imagining Daniel, cowering in a damp Cayuga hut. We seemed to be caught in something larger than us both.

My mother went on. "The night that Captain Bull cried revenge, your father dreamt of Teedyuscung's bear. The next morning, he shaved his head and, armed with his gun, rode with Teedyuscung's son. They attacked the white settlers who, within six moons, had built cabins where Teedyuscung's village used to stand."

My father attacked the settlers' cabins? In pain, I saw him aim his musket at Daniel's cousins. My father fired and I saw flames. Then I saw Daniel's uncle torching Teedyuscung's cabin. I heard screams. I smelled burning flesh. I felt one deep hurt leading to another. Over and over.

"After avenging Teedyuscung's death, your father was not the same," my mother said. "Something in his heart had died. He had always been a peaceful man who would rather hunt than go to war. Now he would spend hours watching leaves float down the river. He would drink white man's rum to ease some deep, unspoken pain. He didn't use his musket again, until age and sickness weakened him.

"He didn't mention the bear, either, although I sensed it stalked him. At night, he'd moan in his sleep. Then you were born and he became himself. Sleeping long and deep, until age and the coughing sickness weakened him."

"Don't go on," I said, not wanting to hear about my father's death.

She stared hard at me. "Coshmoo. You need a spirit from the world beyond—a guardian manitou to give strength and guide you. Go to Broken Stone. Tell him you are a poor boy who needs to face his vision quest. Let Broken Stone prepare you.

"Oh my son. *You dream of bear.*"

CHAPTER
16

———

Clouds shadowed the Susquehanna three nights later as I left Broken Stone's cabin. I needed to find a lonely place in which to hold my vigil. Then I would sing, fast, pray, and hope for a vision in which the Great Creator would reveal my manitou. It could be the spirit of an animal, a rock, a tree; with this manitou to guide me, I could fight off any bear—even if it had mauled a thousand warriors' dreams!

I had fasted all three nights. I had drunk Broken Stone's powerful medicines. My head reeled. Birds became flapping clouds. Leaves blended into trees. My legs were a staggering buck's. They carried me to the Ancient Warrior's grave.

His bones were buried beneath the oldest apple tree. Its gnarled branches formed a sweet-smelling canopy above my head. Its roots cradled my uncertain feet. Daniel and I once had stood among these roots, marveling at the Ancient Warrior's bones. We had whispered prayers as my people had reburied him. I wished Daniel were beside me now. Wishing brought his spirit to nestle in my heart. Its sadness made my insides ache.

His uncle had dragged an unhappy Daniel home. Torn Earlobes, the Cayuga who'd been run off the Seiberts' farm, now wore Daniel's hat, and carried Daniel's gun. My friend had nothing left but an uncle's anger at having to trade three muskets and two kegs of powder for his useless nephew's freedom. Elk Hair, who'd been sent downriver to get Daniel's uncle, had told me this. At the Cayuga village, Elk Hair had seen the blacksmith twist Daniel's ear and say, "You're to have nothing more to do with savages. You understand?"

I hated these ugly words and the frog-faced man who'd said them. Daniel's uncle couldn't keep Daniel and me apart. We'd found bones together. Giant bones. An Ancient Warrior's—

As I stumbled away from the apple tree, I felt the Warrior's thin, hard hand take mine. I heard him singing in my head about a river that would never die. I smelled his apple blossoms. He led me away from my village. I barely reached his shoulder. His silver armbands clinked on his long arms. Within the Ancient Warrior's hand, mine became in turn a beaver's paw, a wolf's, a wildcat's. I was many things, and I was Coshmoo. A friend was leading me.

I found myself at the Chemung River, being lifted up. My head now swam among the clouds. I rode astride a giant water creature's lumbering bones. The

Ancient Warrior, whose hand rested on the water creature's shoulder, asked the Great Creator for a manitou to guide me. He sang of a hard journey that I had to take.

I didn't know where we were going. I didn't care, for I was lost in wonder. The water creature carried me through sunlit meadows, deep green woods and over streams as the Ancient Warrior sang of icy winds, empty bellies, and fire. "Bless Coshmoo," I heard him say. Then they both were gone. And I found myself nestled in soft needles at the base of a friendly fir, halfway up a hill.

I slept. Water trickling in a nearby stream and crows nesting in the tall fir awakened me. The noisy birds, in a large, untidy bowl of twigs and vines, scolded, "Go away! We have babies."

I couldn't go away. Ancient bones had brought me here. A meadow with a small stream stretched out below me. Behind me rose a bristled slope. Rocks and piled earth formed a low wall along the summit. A broken wall. It was an ancient rampart built long ago for a battle waged upon a sacred hill.

Carantouan.

I wanted to leave. I could not. Why had my friends brought me to this hill of dreams and sorrow? Crows scolded me. I hid myself within the shade of the fir's branches. I sang, I fasted, and I prayed that a vision would come soon.

When I wearied of sitting, I stood. When I grew tired of standing, I sat. I slept fitfully, curled like a frightened pup, hidden among branches. Dark turned to daylight five times, transforming the small meadow, patches of thick brush, and the tall tree into dancing shades of green. Carantouan towered at my back. It kept a distant silence. I prayed for a manitou to bless me, but no vision came.

I watched crows soar with the wind, their feathers black against the sky. I wished that I could fly with them. My spirit burned with loneliness. My throat and empty stomach ached. I yearned for even Noh-koomi's indifferent stare. On the sixth day, I made friends with rocks poking out from the blanket of fir needles. I thought a rock would make a powerful manitou. No bear's claw could ever penetrate its skin. I picked up a rock shaped like an arrowhead. I pleaded with this rock to speak.

The rock warmed to my hand. I stared into this warmth and saw a vision of Tioga Point. The smoke from many fires darkened the sky above Tioga. "Rock," I said, relieved that it had spoken, but puzzled by what it was showing me, "why do so many fires burn at Tioga? Only twenty Cayugas live there."

In answer, the smoke began to swirl. It drew into a giant cloud with twenty-six sharp, gleaming teeth. The rock I held grew hot. It burned my hand. This rock was not my manitou. I dropped the rock and it grew fur, four paws, daggered claws. I held my hands against my ears.

Overhead, crows were chattering. Noisy black plumes against a cobalt sky. Light drifted into darkness. Darkness into light. Hungry, frightened, I held my knees and rocked, my back to a sacred hill where wind spirits were whispering, "Your father dreamt of bear. Up the slope is where your father died."

I prayed for a vision in which a guardian manitou would claim me! Eight nights passed. No vision came. My heart became as empty as my belly—gone beyond all aching. It came to me that I would be like other boys who had gone out on a vision quest and come back empty. They lived on, shallow caves. But no bear had ever stalked their dreams. I watched a black ant carry a dead fly over a flat gray rock.

Perhaps, I thought, the Great Creator will send a vision through this ant. An ant would make a powerful manitou. It would take on anything. I said, "Brave ant. You carry a fly three times your size, but you're not frightened or concerned. Will *you* speak to me?"

In answer, small red ants came pouring out of anthills. Hundreds of anthills I hadn't seen! Red ants, like an army, swarmed around the black one. Stung, he died. The red ants carried the black ant and the fly away. As they marched, they fanned out in formation. The formation drew together, becoming two ears. Gleaming teeth. Burning eyes . . .

"No!" I held my head together with my hands, and storm clouds gathered at Carantouan. Wind spirits moaned and the Thunder Beings rumbled. I curled into myself, facing away from the shrouded hill. A rising wind whipped the crows' nest. Rain swept across the little meadow. Large, ugly birds with human heads shot arrows through the sky. I was lonely. Lost. Afraid. I hungered for my Great Creator. And hungering, I pleaded for a manitou. I sang about the fearful bear who'd stalked my dreams.

I sang while wind and rain assailed me. And finally, my singing brought a beam of light. It cut across the sheet of rain. A figure walked slowly down the beam. Walked from the darkened sky down the beam of light to me. As the figure neared, its features became clear: shoulders broad enough to carry restless boys; arms strong enough to pull a warrior's bow; eyes that could see inside a troubled heart. *My father.*

Halfway down the beam, my father stopped. Wet grass greened all around him. Raindrops danced. My legs shook as I stood to greet him. He held out a hand, signing to come no further. His eyes burned bright with love. I longed to run into his strong arms the way I had when I was small, but his hand told me I shouldn't.

He wore a hunting shirt, a breechclout, and leggings of the finest deerskin. Quilled black birds eyed me from his moccasins. Dark wings raised in flight, the birds carried sticks of fire within their beaks. Smoke had blackened my father's face. Sorrow misted the beam of light and the five short steps between us.

My father opened his mouth to speak, and the Thunder Beings roared! Arrows slashed through my father. He stood firm while the earth around us trembled. His eyes burned into mine.

I didn't move, for as I looked in my father's eyes,

117

I saw the vision he was seeing: We stood in a plowed field covered with bleached bones. I saw muskets, pottery shards, pewter spoons, glittering swords, and feathers scattered among bones. I saw a clay pipe resting on a heap of bones. A pipe with a bowl carved into a wolf's head, the totem of my clan.

From somewhere, women wailed. The wailing turned the marrow in my own bones to ice.

Within this vision, my father touched my arm and pointed to the far horizon. A shadow lumbered forth from where the earth met the sky. The shadow grew larger as it neared. Its broad head swayed from side to side. I yearned for Teedyuscung and his musket. Yearned for Daniel and the Ancient Warrior, too. I wanted them to spin with me. Spin with a frightened son and father. The shadow was the bear, and my father's hands were empty.

He had no gun.

The air grew hot with panting. Women screamed. Eyes holding the hunger of a thousand winters glared into mine. My father stepped in front of me. With outstretched hands he fended off the dark bear's slashing teeth. The bear wanted to rip away my father. Feed off me.

But my father wouldn't let him.

In that knowledge, a feeling grew within my heart. It became a flaming sword. I knew that if I, Coshmoo, could grab this sword and wield it, the blade would sear the bear and save my father.

As I reached out to grab the hilt, the Great Creator

118

whispered, "Coshmoo, you're not ready to wield this sword. But look into its shining. See your face."

In silver flames, I saw the circle of my face. Above a lick of hair hovered a protective wing—a shape I'd known from carving pine. A crow. I felt the sudden, warm embrace of wings and the heartbeat of a manitou. *My manitou.*

I slept. Perhaps the bear devoured my father and all the bones within the vision. I don't know. I know only that I awakened to sunlight and a baby crow. A bright-eyed fluff of gray disheveled feathers, he squalled at my nose, demanding to be fed. Fragments of his broken nest lay scattered about him.

I didn't need this little one to assure me of a passage into manhood. The vision had revealed my manitou. The crow was a brave, powerful spirit that I could depend on for the rest of my life. But the Great Creator must have known I needed a friend to journey with through shadows. I named this new friend Wikbi.

CHAPTER 17

———

The corn was man-high, the ears well formed the day the Mohawk messenger rode into our village. Red and black paint streaked his face, and his head was shaved for war. A hot wind whispered through our cornstalks and our apple trees.

Wikbi perched on my shoulder, eyeing the three eagle feathers fluttering in the Mohawk's scalp lock. Wikbi pressed his wing against my cheek. Smart crow. He knew it was unwise to steal feathers from an eagle. The Mohawk nation was a part of the great Iroquois League. Mohawks were mighty warriors.

Our warriors flanked me on all sides. My mother and Broken Stone stood beside the messenger while the women gathered behind the men. The Mohawk began by saying the American rebels had signed a paper declaring independence from their king. They were formally taking up the war hatchet against the British.

This surprised me. For two winters we'd been told

120

the fight between these Americans and the British was like a quarrel between an angry son and his father. Now this quarrel had become a war? Trade goods were already scarce. What hardships would "war" bring?

I wondered if Daniel had found another musket to fight this "war." I hadn't seen him since the Cayugas had taken his other gun. That had been two moons earlier. "Don't go to Sheshequin yet," my mother had told me when I'd returned from Carantouan. "Let Daniel make peace with his uncle."

My mother seemed at peace with me. She was relieved I had a manitou. "Your father is pleased that you've been blessed," she had said. "His spirit no longer haunts me." But I was haunted by my friend.

The Mohawk told us the warriors in his village, a two-day's journey upriver from mine, had decided to join the British. In return, the king promised to protect their homes not only from warring troops, but from hungry settlers as well. Who would protect the Indians living at Tioga Point?

I stroked Wikbi's back, while behind me Bitter Weed grumbled to Bad Shoes about the lack of ammunition. "If war comes to Tioga, we won't be able to defend ourselves," he said.

I thought of McBride's promise to bring ammunition next spring. If only he'd come sooner! Nohkoomi pressed herself against my mother's skirt. My mother cleared her throat. Usually on such occasions, she'd speak through Broken Stone, but not now.

She thanked the Mohawk for his news. She had

121

heard rumors about a war several times throughout the summer. Now she knew them to be true. She asked that the Mohawks not worry themselves over the Delawares at Tioga.

Her next words echoed a song inside me. She said our people would not fight in any white man's war. It would cause too much sorrow. Settlers, whether they took the British or American side, were friends. "After all, we've lived side by side with these settlers for almost a generation now," my mother said. "Our women have shared birthing secrets. Their dead are buried with our dead."

Throughout summer and into fall, drumbeats passed messages about the white man's war from one village to the next along the Susquehanna and the Chemung. They said British and American armies both swarmed across the land. They tore corn from stalks. They trampled squash. They picked all the apples from the trees. They stormed trading posts, taking rifles, muskets, lead, powder—anything they needed in the fight involving freedom.

These armies didn't come near us, but neither did trade goods. Bitter Weed, Bad Shoes, and Spotted Owl canoed downriver to the Wyoming Valley—a two-night journey. They found no ammunition at Hollenback's store, and the shoes and blankets were gone—all sent to American troops.

My powder keg was nearly empty. I had only seven bullets left. Every time dogs howled, I hoped they announced a trader's arrival. But none came. "If we had sided with the British king, he would have seen to our needs," Bitter Weed told my mother several times.

"If we had sided with the British, I'd be binding wounds and mourning the dead instead of braiding corn husks," my mother told me. She was plaiting the husks together to hang from our rafters. With wet sinew, I was lashing flint arrowheads to dogwood shafts. I was tired of making arrows. Tired of hunting with a bow. But like others, I'd had to save my powder and lead to protect our neutral village, and for the deer hunt in late fall.

My mother hummed as she braided. The tune was that of a white man's song she'd learned when we lived in Sheshequin. It was a sad song, about the man who'd hung upon the cross. It made me want to go downriver and melt into shadows around a cabin built into a hill. There I'd wait until I saw my friend whose hair stood up like mine.

But earlier, when I'd mentioned Daniel, my mother had said, "For seven nights, I've heard the screech owl cry. This omen of death comes from the south. Do not go to Sheshequin yet."

Shrill cries broke through my mother's humming. Not a screech owl's—they were Wikbi's cries. They rode the wind coming through our window. "Wikbi and Nohkoomi hunt together," my mother said.

"No," I replied. "Wikbi always hunts alone. His cries tell me he has caught a mouse!"

"When you're hunting with Elk Hair, Wikbi hunts with Nohkoomi. I've watched them."

I'd had Wikbi for almost four moons. I thought I knew everything about him, from his happy dance when I returned from hunting, to his caws of alarm when strangers came, to the hollow in the burned sycamore where he stored his treasures—shiny stones, bits of mica, and a brass bead he'd stolen from my mother.

I ran outside to prove her wrong. Downhill from our cabin, Wikbi swooped, shrieking as he attacked a rock pile. A patch of gray wiggled through laurel branches next to it. I couldn't believe what I was seeing! Nohkoomi, using her forelegs, inched her belly along the graveled ground. Her yellow eyes never left the small fury of my attacking crow.

I hid behind a maple and watched Nohkoomi move closer to the rock pile until her nose was three paw-lengths away. There, head lowered, she waited. My head grew dizzy with Wikbi's shrieks. A chipmunk's head must have grown dizzy, too. For suddenly, the little one dashed out from a crack between the rocks. Nohkoomi's large jaws snapped him up!

Then came the strangest part. For me, it was beyond belief. Nohkoomi dropped the chipmunk. She gazed at it proudly, as a hunter would his prey. Wikbi landed in front of her. He pranced like a little warrior, back and forth, and watched Nohkoomi eat the chipmunk's head and forelegs.

Nohkoomi backed away. Wikbi cocked his head, as if to say, "You're done?" Nohkoomi whined and

Wikbi took the remaining carcass by its tail. On young wings, he lifted off the ground. I shielded my eyes and watched in amazement as he carried the chipmunk into burning sunlight. It looked as if he carried fire.

I found my little warrior later, outside White Fawn's cabin. He perched on the rim of a storage basket she was decorating. His dark head bobbed up and down as White Fawn painted circles on the ash splints.

"Wikbi likes baskets," White Fawn said. "They remind him of birds' nests."

"He likes eating chipmunks, too." I told White Fawn how Wikbi hunted with my mother's dog.

White Fawn said, "Nohkoomi and Wikbi are so different. Wikbi's cheeky. Full of mischief. He stole mica I was working into pottery." She tapped Wikbi's beak with the dry end of her paint stick. "Nohkoomi seems so serious. All ribs and hungry yellow eyes. I think Wikbi will be good for Nohkoomi. He will keep her happy and well fed.

"Look at him now. He struts back and forth along my basket rim. So full of himself. Cheeky bird." She moved her paint stick in time to Wikbi's bobbing head. "Oh, but Coshmoo, one of his tail feathers is torn! You must warn him not to be too cocky when he hunts. Crows get hurt."

She looked at me as she was speaking. I felt my face grow hot. I turned away and saw a flock of startled blackbirds peppering the sky above her. I pointed to them. "Someone's coming!"

"I hope it's a trader," White Fawn said. "Just

before you came, I asked Wikbi if the effort I spent weaving and painting baskets would return to me in a trader's thick blankets. Ours are worn thin."

"What did Wikbi say?"

"Sweet bird. He said, 'With a basket as beautiful as this? Of course.' "

Above us a cloud of blackbirds rose and fell. Dogs began to howl. Cawing alarm, Wikbi flew away. The visitor whom the blackbirds had been heralding was here. I prayed it was a trader. I needed ammunition.

I raced to the village clearing, White Fawn's footsteps tailing me. My mother, Nohkoomi at her side, shielded her eyes from a piercing sun. Mounted horses milled in front of her, scattering women who'd been pounding corn. Shouting boys, like flocks of birds, poured in from the cattle fields.

"Oh, Coshmoo. Look!" White Fawn grabbed my arm. A gleaming coal-black stallion reared. Red ribbons braided through his mane fluttered against the sky. I would have loved to own this horse. He pawed the sky, then danced, his muscled hindquarters damp with sweat. He pranced sideways and I saw his rider's face. Red and black war paint crossed a long straight nose. Two flat, dark eyes glared down this nose. This was no trader bringing ammunition. This was Flying Wolf.

CHAPTER
18

———

Silver brooches lined the black stallion's bridle. They reflected sunlight the way White Fawn's eyes reflected the glory of my cousin who now reined in this handsome horse. Her look of admiration made my heart turn cold.

A new tattoo snaked down Flying Wolf's forearm and darkened the back of his right hand. Whoever had needled this tattoo knew the spirit of the timber rattler: the beauty of its diamond back, the violence of its sudden fangs.

Flying Wolf thrust a musket above his head and shouted greetings to our men. Bitter Weed raised his arm and shouted back. A large bay horse sidled into Flying Wolf's stallion. The stallion lashed out. The bay whirled. Torn Earlobes, the Cayuga who'd taken Daniel's hat, was riding it! He glanced at me with narrowed eyes. His head was shaved for war. As was my cousin's. As were the heads of all twelve other horsemen. Two of these men, although dressed and painted like Indians, were white.

Flying Wolf sat on my bed, pouring gunpowder from a large leather bag into his powder horn. From her spot near the fireplace, Nohkoomi watched him with wary eyes. Wikbi perched on my father's musket while I sat on a bearskin rug and angrily lashed arrowheads to shafts. I resented the powder and lead that Flying Wolf had. I needed it for hunting. And for protecting my village from men like him.

Flying Wolf rode with displaced Tories, those Americans who sided with the British, and a scattering of warriors from different tribes—Cayugas, Mohawks, and Senecas. These warriors had become part of what Flying Wolf called "Colonel Butler's Rangers." Flying Wolf said this Colonel Butler was very rich. He gave his men all the ammunition they needed in return for scalps taken from American rebels. Colonel Butler had grown quite fond of Flying Wolf. He'd given him the stallion that filled White Fawn's eyes with wonder.

"You will take no scalps from any American living downriver from me," my mother told Flying Wolf. She sat beside me, her tense hands weaving a basket made of spruce roots. "Neither you, nor your Iroquois, nor your white friends are to harm them. Nephew. Are your ears listening? These Americans are my friends. They live within *my* shadow."

Her shadow, cast by firelight, looked large. Her words felt even larger. But Flying Wolf wasn't cowed by them. He said, "Colonel Butler tells us the Wyoming Valley is General Washington's breadbasket. Colonel Butler says we must burn all the farms that supply these troops with corn and wheat. He pays us well." My cousin's arrogance thickened the air like smoke.

"Colonel Butler this. Colonel Butler that. Does my proud nephew now take orders from a white man?" my mother asked.

"*Colonel Butler* says to keep our muskets trained on the Oneidas, the Tuscaroras, and the Delawares as well. Rumors say they may be leaning to the rebels' side." Flying Wolf capped his powder horn and glared at me.

I rose. I stood over my mother. I made our shadows merge into one that was even larger and more powerful. "Perhaps my people, the Delawares, would be wise to keep their muskets trained on their Seneca cousins," I said, surprising myself with this bold response. "Rumors say the Senecas lean to the British side."

Flying Wolf rose from my bed.

"Bah!" My mother spat into the fire and stood, placing herself between us. "I hate your Colonel Butler! I hate this white man's war! It tries to pit one tribe against the other. Flying Wolf! Coshmoo! Look at me!" My mother took out her knife. Making certain we were watching, she drew the blade across her palm.

I watched blood well in her hand and was afraid to speak. A woman can cause a river to run backward. Make the corn grow tall. A woman creates life and, if angered, can just as easily destroy it. Even a mother can be unpredictable, like summer storms.

She covered the knife blade with her blood, then buried the handle in our earthen floor. "Imagine it's winter and this knife sticks up from a sheet of ice. Tell me, Flying Wolf: What happens when a starving wolf comes upon it?"

Flying Wolf shrugged, looking as uneasy with the question as I felt.

"Hungry for the taste of blood, he licks the blade and cuts his tongue," my mother said. "His blood, the pain, his tongue, now frozen to the knife blade—all make him crazy. He tries to dislodge the knife. His starving pack circles as he thrashes. Flecks of blood stain the snow. Finally, hunger drives the pack beyond knowing that the wounded wolf is their brother. They attack. They fight each other over his blood. And in this fight, the pack destroys itself—all because of a single knife.

"Don't you see?" She stared at Flying Wolf and me. "Men like Colonel Butler plant a knife blade with the riches they promise you if you fight their white man's war. They bait the blade with the blood from old wounds and treacheries. Then they sit back and watch you kill each other."

"I've never heard of wolves attacking a wounded brother," said Flying Wolf.

"It's an old story, passed on to me by a Huron who lives in the north. Heed my words, both of you. We must stay neutral in the white man's war or . . . we will die."

Flying Wolf laughed uneasily.

"Don't attack the Americans living near me, nephew," my mother repeated. "They live within the shadow of my wings."

"The Americans who live along the Susquehanna's west branch don't." Flying Wolf flung open the door. He let in the scent of nervous horses, white men's voices, and smoke. Not from cooking fires, but from the hot coals his friends were using to melt lead for bullets.

For an instant, sunlight blazing through the open door blinded me. I recalled Wikbi, on proud young wings, flying into such a light. It had looked as if he carried fire. The door drifted shut, and I told my mother, "In spite of Daniel's uncle and omens, I must go downriver. I must warn our friends about Flying Wolf."

I expected her resistance. She'd heard the screech owl cry. Hands trembling—with fear or anger, I couldn't tell—she filled a pouch with white oak bark. Handing it to me, she said, "Coshmoo. Keep your eyes open. Watch for cougars. And give this bark to Daniel's mother. Tell her my white oak tea will bring strength back to her husband. Tell my friends that Queen Esther says a fearful wind blows from the north. It would be wise for them to bolt their doors and keep their windows shut."

CHAPTER
19

—◆—

Gickokwita's rays blazed off the descending axe. I shaded my eyes as I crouched within a cave of willows and watched Daniel cut logs from a downed tree. In the four moons since I'd seen him, Daniel had grown taller. I wondered if he'd grown inside as well. Did he now have a manitou, too?

Tree branches fanned out from the riverbank and into the meadow where Naomi played. Daniel's sister sang as she chased white butterflies circling clumps of blue flowers. Her voice was gentle, unlike the bark of voices coming from the Seiberts' cabin. I sensed the presence of maybe eight, nine white men.

These harsh voices made me hesitate to come out from hiding. They made me think that Flying Wolf had already been here. But he couldn't have been. He had left my village just before I did. I had followed him. Whooping and hollering, he and the rangers had headed west, not south.

Cattle lowed, moving slowly through meadow

grass Flying Wolf would have burned if he'd been here; they grabbed at the tasseled stalks. A crow's shadow winged across the willows. One of Wikbi's brothers. I'd left Wikbi safely tethered to the shelf above my bed.

Daniel rested his hands on the axe handle and stared at mud-packed roots. His eyes turned soft with dreams. I sensed a longing in them for another place and time. I recalled dark clay and bone. A giant water creature's eye.

In spite of gunfire, I stepped out from the willows. Keeping low to the ground, I let tall grass hide me. Naomi stopped singing when she saw me. She ran to her brother and wrapped her arms around his legs. A look of alarm crossed Daniel's face. It changed to recognition and delight. "Coshmoo!"

I signed to Daniel a happy greeting, but I approached him slowly, not wanting to frighten the little girl whose arms held him close. Naomi hadn't seen me for six moons. She watched me now with startled eyes.

I crouched before her and fluttered my hands through sunlight, casting a dancing shadow on the ground.

"Butterfly." She giggled.

I formed a long-eared body and made it hop.

"Rabbit," Naomi said.

I bridged my thumbs and flapped my hands, slow and steady.

"A crow!" Naomi released her brother and knelt beside me. "Look!" With three fingers, she made the

133

outline of a duck's head and made it quack. I laughed and through my laughter heard again the bark of voices.

"No one must see you!" Daniel pulled me into the hollow of earth formed by the uprooted tree. "What are you doing here?" His voice had turned anxious.

"I brought a message from my mother." I wanted to break the news about Flying Wolf gently, especially with Naomi here. She watched me cast the shadow of a fox, slipping through trees.

"You shouldn't have come."

"Because of your uncle?"

Daniel winced. "He whipped me. He said, 'This is only a taste of what you'll get if you ever go near a savage again.' "

"Your father should have stopped him!"

"My father is not well." High-pitched flutes began to play. The shrill notes came from the left of Daniel's cabin, near his uncle's blacksmith's shed. Drumbeats replaced the barking voices. Not the mellowed beat of hands, but the hard pounding of sticks against taut deerskin.

"It's my uncle's militia. Drilling." A loud voice sounded. Its words were muffled, but I could hear the harshness in them. The tramp of marching feet, the slap of hands against gun stocks, and the sudden roar of musket fire made me feel trapped.

"The muskets aren't loaded." Daniel grabbed my arm, as if he feared that I might flee.

"Do you have ammunition for these muskets?"

"A little. Powder and lead are hard to get."

"Keep them loaded. Flying Wolf is back."

Daniel's face paled. His fingers tightened around my arm. A beetle scurried along a muddy root. Naomi poked the beetle with a stick.

Afraid that even the wind had ears, I whispered, "My cousin rides with a handful of Tories and nine warriors from different tribes. Allied with a Colonel Butler, they attack farms along the Susquehanna's west branch. My mother has warned them to stay away from you. But keep your eyes open. Your doors barred. Your muskets ready."

Daniel replied, "Five nights ago, Tories attacked a farm only two hills east of ours. They burned it down! They killed three of our friends!"

Omens of death. A screech owl's cry. My mother was right. "You shouldn't stay here." I told him.

"Neither should you. My uncle imagines Delawares with raised war hatchets, hiding in the brush. At night, he thinks he hears your moccasins. Fearing another massacre, he tells his militia to keep their muskets trained on Tioga Point."

Gunfire accompanied these words. Smoke clouded the air. With her stick, Naomi drew a circle in the mud beneath our feet—one curve leading into another.

"My people can't leave Tioga Point. It's our home. It's our link with the sea." As I said these words, my hands took flight, casting shadows: a giant water creature's lumbering, the Ancient Warrior's clicking dance, a leaping shad, my father's hands.

A bear.

"My family can't leave Sheshequin," Daniel said. "This farm is all we have."

I looked into his eyes. And within their depths I saw his farm: its meadowed hill, its grazing cattle, a cabin snug against a flowered slope, a blacksmith's shed.

"I love this river," he said. "I love this valley and its hills. I love its bones! I won't let the British, the Tories, your cousin—I won't let anyone take them away from me.

"And I won't let talk of war and massacres come between us, either." Daniel's blue eyes glimmered.

"But we can't see each other again. The path between our homes grows too thick with briers," I said. "Militias march. Flying Wolf is back."

"Three miles upriver, near that island where we used to swim, a wide-mouthed creek enters the Susquehanna," Daniel said.

"I know this creek."

"A large sycamore grows on the south side of the creek mouth. The east side of the tree is split and the inside of the tree is hollow to the height of a full-grown man. We could meet there. On the morning after each full moon. We could hide inside it. No one would see us."

"Once the leaves have fallen, I'll be at our winter hunting grounds. For maybe a moon. And when the snow comes . . ."

"Inside this tree, there's a hard strip of wood whitened by fire," said Daniel. "When we can't meet, we'll write messages there, whatever may be in our hearts. If what we wish to say is urgent—"

"I'll caw outside your window—a crow's warning. Seven caws. That means, 'Meet me at our sycamore.'"

"Yes. And I'll do the same for you."

"Daniel. Do you ever dream of bear?" I signed the rolling motion a bear makes when running.

"No. I dream of General Washington." The look I liked crossed Daniel's face. It spoke to me of visions. Made me think that Daniel was more Indian than white. "He wears black boots and rides a grand white horse. I see him galloping on this horse. The longer the horse gallops, the larger it grows. Its pounding feet leave hoofprints in the mud along the Susquehanna. They form pond holes in meadows and hollow caves in hills."

"Such a powerful man," I said. "Perhaps he can help me." It was then I told Daniel about the stalking fear even my vision quest had not erased—the dark bear who carried in his burning eyes the hunger of a thousand winters. "I must shoot this bear. Somehow. Or this bear will kill me." I realized the frightening truth in these words even as I said them.

CHAPTER
20

―――◆―――

When I left Daniel's farm, Bitter Weed and Bad Shoes were waiting for me just around the river's bend. Their canoe slipped out from the cover of a fallen tree to come alongside mine. They carried no lines, no nets, no spears for fishing. I saw no signs that they'd been hunting, and my belly turned cold. *They'd followed me.*

I greeted them. They nodded. They said nothing. The silence, broken only by the dip of paddles, bristled with unspoken questions. "Coshmoo. What were you doing at the Seiberts' farm? Bringing news about Flying Wolf and Butler's Rangers to white settlers? Acting as a spy?"

The Susquehanna splashed against my bow. I dug my paddle in and angled across the current. Bitter Weed and Bad Shoes kept their canoe next to mine. I glided into a pool of quiet water and said to Bitter Weed's unsmiling face, "Daniel's father is sick. My mother had me bring him white oak tea."

Bitter Weed grunted, his eyes appraising me.

"An American militia practices at Daniel's farm." I hoped this bit of information might appease him. "There were eight, maybe nine white men."

"We know. We heard their muskets." Bitter Weed's muscled arms gleamed as he slowly paddled in the bow.

"The muskets weren't loaded. The Americans save their ammunition for fighting off Tories. Like us, they've had trouble getting powder and lead." I wanted to tell this warrior something he didn't know.

"Flying Wolf told us the same. He said the British have no trouble getting ammunition. If we join Colonel Butler, he'll give us what we need."

"So will McBride." I said, looking from Bitter Weed to Bad Shoes. "The trader's coming in the spring. He'll have ammunition for us."

"And how are we to pay for it?" Bad Shoes held his paddle up as if it were a musket. He aimed it at a fat gray rock and pretended to pull a trigger. "McBride wants beaver pelts. Our ponds have been outtrapped. They're empty."

"Not all of them," I replied, now paddling hard to keep up with these men. Bad Shoes angled his paddle in the current. Bitter Weed dug in. As their canoe shot away from mine, I called after them, "I know of a pond that teems with beaver!"

One moon later, we were at our winter hunting quarters—fifteen men, six boys, and the three women who'd come with us to butcher deer. Backs huddled against the wind, we warmed our hands above a smoldering fire. Our faces were gray with cold and disappointment. In the sixteen nights that we'd been hunting, we had killed only five deer; Red Hawk was complaining. He'd used up his powder. His bullets, too. And so little meat to show for it! Bad Shoes told Red Hawk not to worry. He'd get ammunition from McBride. In the spring. He looked at me and said to everyone, "Coshmoo knows of a pond that holds enough beaver to supply us with ammunition until our Elder Brother Moon should die."

"Where is this pond?" Red Hawk asked.

"It's hidden," I said, "in a narrow valley west of Horsehead's Path."

He laughed at me. "That area was outtrapped long ago."

"The beaver have come back."

"You mistake settlers for beaver." Bitter Weed stared across burning logs at me. "They swarm through our hunting grounds. They frighten all the game away."

"My pond has five lodges and over fifty beaver!"

"*Fifty* beaver?" Bitter Weed snorted. He pretended something had caught in his throat, and began to choke. Bad Shoes pounded him on the back. Soon everyone was laughing.

That night, I couldn't sleep. It was too cold. Branches clawed against the hut I shared with Elk Hair. He was snoring. Wrapped in my blanket, I thought: I'll take Bad Shoes, Red Hawk, and Bitter Weed to my father's pond. In late winter, when the pelts are ripe. I'll prove to them that I speak the truth. Their eyes will widen with surprise at the sight of so many beaver. But I won't let them take too many. Only enough to buy the ammunition we need. And we'll leave at least one lodge intact.

"Always leave at least one lodge," my father had said. How he had loved our little brothers of the water. I remembered basking with him on a hot and peaceful afternoon. Pond water lapped against a beaver lodge. Our little brothers sprawled on top, combing their claws through fur that held a summer sheen of blue. Smiling gently, my father had pointed to a mother beaver nursing babies. "She's the reason we must keep this pond a secret from hungry trappers like the white man. They'd trap everything. They'd leave no beaver to bear young."

I knew my father would have been pleased with my careful trapping. I'd taken few females. The winter before I'd trapped none. Now there were five lodges, where once there'd been only one.

Snow was falling the day we returned from hunting deer. Those who'd stayed in our village to tend the fires and cattle hid their disappointment at the small amount of meat we had brought. "We still have corn, dried fish, sugar cakes, and milk," they said. "And the six sacks of white man's flour, ten chickens, and three hogs that Flying Wolf brought.

"While you were gone," they said, "Flying Wolf visited us after raiding cabins east of Shickellamy's town. Flying Wolf is rich and generous. He's given us not only food, but two kettles, five blankets, seven knives, and three bars of lead. Flying Wolf has given White Fawn a fine necklace of blue glass beads."

"He shouldn't have given it to her. He had no right," I told my mother later. I was melting Flying Wolf's bars of lead in a cast-iron kettle, to make bullets. But the bullets wouldn't do me any good until I had gunpowder. He should have brought powder instead of beads.

"White Fawn won't speak to me. She won't even look at me. The village is full of marriage talk," I said, waiting for the lead to heat until it flowed like river water. Then I'd add the ball of fat to clarify it. I couldn't wait to do this. The fat made the lead turn angry. Made it boil—the way I felt inside.

My mother laughed. "Your cousin courts White Fawn, but marriage? It's still far away. His courting is not the reason she avoids you."

"Then what is?" I tossed a dry wood splinter into the liquid lead. The splinter blackened but didn't catch fire. The lead was ready.

A soft expression crossed my mother's face. "White Fawn isn't permitted to talk to any man. White Fawn is a woman now. Less than one moon ago, she faced her first seclusion."

I thought of the secluded hut that sheltered women for several nights each moon. It was a part of women

I'd heard about but didn't understand—this blood of life that flowed between a woman's legs. It cast strange spells. It held a power as deep as the mysteries of Carantouan. White Fawn? A woman? I added fat to the melted lead and it boiled. Smoke poured out, stinking up the cabin.

Wikbi squawked. His wings beat through the smoke. My mother coughed and raced outside with Wikbi and Nohkoomi right behind her.

The smoke didn't bother me. I skimmed the dross off the boiling lead, thinking all the while of White Fawn. I didn't like that she'd become a woman. It set her apart. Now she'd have to hide her face from men and boys—except those who courted her. Like Flying Wolf. I hated him. Hated the sound of his name. Everyone talked about "Flying Wolf."

I poured molten lead into my bullet mold and the thought came to me that in three moons the name Coshmoo could be on everyone's lips. Because Coshmoo's beaver pelts could buy ammunition for the men. And brightly colored cloth for the women. And maybe pretty silver bells for White Fawn. She'd like them.

That night, the snow stopped falling—a good omen, I thought. The full moon rose. And then, a bear shadow crossed my window. For a while I kept watch, fearing it might come again. When I finally slept, the bear clawed at the cabin walls within my dreams.

The next morning, I canoed downriver to keep my promise to meet Daniel. I wanted to talk to him. But he wasn't at our sycamore tree. For the first time, I stood inside the tree. The sun lit the gray-white streak on which Daniel had charcoaled an army of twig-shaped men. These men must have become as rich as Flying Wolf, for each carried a musket, bullet pouch, and powder horn. A proud man rode the large horse that was leading them. I knew this man had to be Daniel's General Washington.

In red ochre I drew nine ears of corn and only three deer heads to let Daniel know corn kept our bellies full, but deer were scarce. I drew a picture of a trader with full packs to tell Daniel of our hope and need. I did not draw my father's beaver pond or the men I planned to take there.

Beneath General Washington, I drew the outline of a bear. As I did, the sycamore seemed to enfold me. Its spirit protected my back, while Gickokwita's golden feathers stroked my face. I wondered if, when Daniel stood inside this tree, he felt such warmth. Maybe that was why he had chosen it as our meeting place. The tree smelled of Daniel—a mix of wood smoke, white man's bread, and sunlight off pale skin.

CHAPTER
21

⬥

E verything the beaver does, it does well," Bitter Weed said. His words formed clouds in the biting air as we drove our stakes into the water spill of the beaver's dam. We'd positioned the stakes close together so that even the smallest beaver couldn't escape. Elk Hair, Bad Shoes, and Half Moon, spears and clubs piled at their feet, joked on shore as they waited for us to finish. Nearby, dogs sprawled in the frozen grass.

"Not only does the beaver form clever dams and lodges, but his sleek fur brings us swords, hatchets, bullet molds, lead, and powder," Bitter Weed continued, his words moving to the rhythm of a pounding I found hard to follow. My hands were numb from driving stakes, as was my heart. I'd planned on bringing three men to my father's pond. Anxious for arms and powder, fourteen had come.

"One beaver pelt used to bring a half a pound of powder. Now it takes two." Bitter Weed glanced approvingly at the large ice-coated pond. Timber, downed by beaver, lay scattered along the banks. From where we stood, we could see four of the five lodges, each one taller than Bitter Weed. "There are enough beaver here to bring us three kegs full of powder," he said.

"Ten!" Bad Shoes called from shore. "And bars of lead as well!"

None of these men had believed in the largesse of the beaver pond. They did now. A cold wind tore at my furred robe. Fighting off the chill, I clenched my teeth and pounded my last stake into the spill. I felt Bitter Weed appraising me. Ever since he'd caught me at the river bend near Daniel's farm, he'd viewed me with suspicious eyes. He thought that I, Coshmoo, was a traitor to our people. Bitter Weed was wrong.

"We'd better take many beaver," he said, throwing his hammer onshore. "Armies swarm out of winter quarters now. War clouds darken the sky. This spring may be the last time we see a trader who wants pelts."

Broken Stone, who'd been with other men readying canoes, stepped out onto a spit of land upwind from us. Steep, wooded slopes rose behind him. He held up an open hand and let the wind carry crumbled tobacco leaves across the frozen water while he sang to our little brothers, asking that they honor us with many pelts.

There was a sadness to Broken Stone's song, as if he sensed impending sorrow. I sensed it, too. But we had to fill our powder kegs, and we needed lead. Muskets were useless without ammunition. McBride was coming soon.

Now that the stakes were driven into the dam, canoes carrying men with axes and spears cut through thin ice toward four lodges built of mud-slabbed limbs, water weeds, and swamp grass. Inside these lodges slept my little brothers of the water. Winter trees stood stark against the sky. Cutting through their jagged shadows, the canoes drew closer. Closer still. My stomach cramped. Red Hawk whooped. He drove an axe into a beaver lodge.

I heard the dull sound of frightened beaver diving deep. The bearskin robe I wore could not keep out the wind as I stood next to Bitter Weed on the beaver dam. Chilled, I gripped my club and watched dark shapes flee through the icy water.

Yelping dogs raced through the brush and reeds that surrounded my father's pond. Two dogs stopped. Wagging their tails, they sniffed a mat of whitened grass and whined. Elk Hair joined them and stamped along the sod, listening for the hollow sound that meant the presence of an escape tunnel leading to the water's edge. He drove in stakes to block it. Bad Shoes kicked aside the whining dogs and with his stake tore a hole into the tunnel. He held his spear poised and ready for a frightened beaver to surface.

A whiskery nose, then a glossy back broke the water that lapped the mud-packed poplar trunks on which I stood. Beside me, Bitter Weed tensed. Before he had a chance to thrust his spear, I did something I'd watched my father do. I plunged my arm into the icy water, grabbed the fighting beaver by his tail, and pulled him out. It was a grandfather beaver. Large and fat. He twisted violently, teeth bared, trying to slash me. I swiftly clubbed him. His struggling died. I felt his proud song enter my heart. It spoke to me of sun-baked hours spent basking on a lodge; of poplar trunks giving way beneath sharp teeth; of the coolness of pond water ruddered by a large flat tail.

I sang back to this brave beaver as I placed his heavy, sleek-furred body carefully on shore. My song spoke of meat—roasted, smoked, pounded with dried fruit; of pelts, tanned and made into robes and white-man's hats; of bones that I would return to the pond so that no dogs or wolves could dishonor them. Nothing would be wasted.

I noted Bitter Weed's approving grunt when I stepped back onto the dam. This grunt made me feel good. I began to think that maybe one day I would be a warrior like Bitter Weed. After all, I had battled a fierce beaver with bare hands to bring my people ammunition. And I had treated the beaver with respect.

After that, each time I clubbed a beaver, I felt a little better. Inside, I grew bigger and more powerful, for I thought about other needed goods these pelts would bring: blankets, new hunting knives, and pistols. Soon, I had no time to sing. Only to spear and club. Red Hawk ran from one body to the next, exclaiming over the beauty of the soft, dense fur.

Four broken lodges now littered the icy water. Blood, broken timbers, and brown pelted bodies darkened the frosty shore. We'd taken enough. But Bitter Weed looked at me expectantly. He wanted more. I did, too. I was lost. Glutted on pride, the strong scent of beaver, and now, a hot, fat dream of what the extra pelts might bring—tooled armbands, a gentleman's buttoned coat, and tall black boots that would make me look as fine as Flying Wolf. And bells. I wanted silver bells for White Fawn.

And so, I led Bitter Weed to the fifth lodge. It was tucked tightly against a bank and hidden by overhanging willows. Once, seated beside my father, I'd watched a mother beaver comb her hair atop this lodge. I'd listened to a mother beaver sing a love song to her young.

Saplings broke beneath our feet as we climbed onto this last lodge. Our shadows reached across the whitened maze of old roots and birch and poplar branches. My heavy robe made my shadow look broader and more powerful than Bitter Weed's. Our breath misted the fragile air. Beneath our feet, a beaver family hid within beds of soft grass and fine wood chips. I used Elk Hair's axe to tear apart their lodge. I thrust my spear into a fleeing body. The beaver fought to swim free. I pinned it against a fallen log until it died. It was a mother beaver. Fat with young.

CHAPTER 22

———◆———

You've captured the song," White Fawn said. It was the first time in the three moons since she'd become a woman that she'd spoken to me. In hands stained by the walnuts she'd been shelling, she held my wooden crow. I'd carved the eyes anew, for the bold expression in them had been wrong. This crow was no warrior.

"The crow's eyes sing with pain," she said. "They sadden me."

"Crow went beyond what he should have done. Fire blackened his feathers. Fire singed his song. These are reasons to feel pain."

"Yes, but there's beauty to the song as well. I see it here, where sunlight reflects off his wings." For the first time in three moons, White Fawn's eyes met mine.

"There's no beauty in Crow's song."

"It's here! I see it. I feel it." White Fawn fingered Crow's right wing. She ran her palm along his chest. It felt as if she touched me.

"Your mother told me what happened at the beaver pond," she said softly. "Crows make mistakes. But they have caring hearts as well. Deep inside, they want to help their people." White Fawn handed me the crow. Our fingers met. Her thoughtful eyes grazed mine. At that moment, I wanted to give White Fawn everything—the earth, the sky, the sea.

More than ever, now, I waited for McBride. That spring, it always seemed to rain. The shad came late, and there weren't as many as before. Too raw to move, I didn't canoe the swollen Susquehanna to see a friend or to draw pictures in a tree. Nor did I fish for Red Eyes, roam the woods with Wikbi, or hunt with Elk Hair. I kept my head tucked beneath my wing.

As I waited, I carved seven little beaver out of walnut, for I wanted to recapture a song that I had silenced. I named them, from the fat one I called Grandfather down to the smallest, Nitschu. I lined them up on the shelf above my bed.

One night, I dreamt about the grandfather beaver I had carved. The bear with the hunger of a thousand winters grabbed Grandfather by his tail. He lifted him high into the snow-filled air. Grandfather struggled to escape. And suddenly, I was standing on the beaver dam, facing the bear. I was screaming, "You've taken enough!" I screamed and screamed, until I screamed myself awake.

Beaver pelts, stretched on hoops, waited for the British trader. And waited. Finally, as the women prepared the ground for planting corn, drums began to beat from one village to another. They said McBride, with a pack train of five strong mules, was in the Cherry Valley. His mules carried powder, lead, bullet molds, knives, blankets, beads, and more. Everyone in my village anticipated their arrival. Now McBride was in Unadilla. Now in Onoquaga. He'd be coming to Tioga soon. I hoped his mules held all the goods we'd need until both sun and moon should die. Never again did I want to hunt for beaver.

"Sorrow won't return the beaver to your father's pond," my mother said several times. "What's done is done. Think of what the pelts will buy."

McBride arrived in fog and rain. I was certain I saw five mules, lined up one behind the other. Five mules meant five times as many trader's packs as McBride had brought before. This would bring a happy song to many hearts. Elk Hair and I called out to McBride, offering to help him unpack his mules.

"Mules?" he called back. "I've brought but one. The others are with the Mohawks at Unadilla and Onoquaga. Stubborn mules. They wouldn't budge another inch. They were too worn-out from slogging through the mud. You can help unload the one I have."

I sweetened my disappointment by thinking that the white mule who brayed at us was McBride's strongest. This long-eared mule could carry at least four kegs of powder and several heavy packs.

But the four canvas bags Elk Hair and I carried into Broken Stone's cabin weren't as heavy as they should have been. And there was but one small powder keg. The crowded cabin turned thick with worried glances.

Where were all the trade goods McBride had promised us?

He removed his mud-stained blanket coat and exchanged solemn greetings with Broken Stone. His green eyes glanced from one man to another. Rain, dripping from a leak in Broken Stone's roof, landed on McBride's cheek. He wiped the rain away. His eyes would not meet mine.

"He hasn't brought half of what he'd promised," Elk Hair whispered to me.

McBride cleared his throat. His worn deerskin shirt looked as muddy as his coat. While rain began to beat against the roof, he told us how happy he was to be our trader. He hoped to see us often. His scarred hands signed regret that he hadn't brought all the goods he'd promised. Gunpowder was scarce and so hard to keep dry. He'd have to charge four times what he'd charged last spring. But the powder he'd brought contained twice the firing power of any he had ever used. After all, the king himself had blessed it.

He said that in order to get lead, he'd had to fight off an army of American rebels to board a British ship. To secure bullet molds, he'd had to face a flood. As for knives, the blacksmiths' shops were empty. War, he said, made everything so difficult.

"Drumbeats told us you led a pack train of five mules," Broken Stone said.

"And these mules carried many kegs of powder. Stacks of lead. New knives and muskets," Bitter Weed added.

Beside me, Elk Hair whispered loudly, "Drumbeats said McBride brought silver gorgets, swords, and axes as well."

"All of this is true." McBride rubbed the scars that webbed out from his red bandanna. His eyes darted from one angry-looking man to the next. I wondered if they took in the thinness of our blankets, our broken-edged knives, our empty kegs.

"But Mohawks bought most of these things before I could bring them here. I had to offer them the trade goods first. After all, they're friends with my chief, Colonel Butler. They're allied with the king."

Broken Stone kept his face like granite. We'd been waiting for these trade goods throughout the winter. All my father's beaver had been killed to get them.

"You promised to bring the ammunition we needed!" I told McBride after a bitter session of bargaining. We were hurrying through rain to a meal my mother was preparing in our cabin.

"I tried."

"You didn't! You saved only one small powder keg for us. I thought you were our friend." I opened the door to the scent of broth and Wikbi's welcoming screech.

"War makes trade goods scarce." McBride rubbed his hand along his forehead, as if it pained him.

"War turns friends into traitors," I said, thinking of a spy whose name sounded like an echo.

For the first time that day, McBride's eyes met mine. They flashed like gunpowder in a frizzen pan. "What have you done to stop this war that turns friends into traitors?"

"It's a white man's war, not ours," I said, caught with McBride between the rain and the scent-filled room in which I ate and slept and dreamt. My mother watched us. Listening.

"It is everyone's war!" He pushed up his sleeve. A strange tattoo of two men, an Indian and white man, their arms locked around each other, darkened the inside of his arm.

CHAPTER
23

I stared at McBride. He stared at me. My mother's approaching moccasins whispered through the pound of rain. Wikbi alighted on my shoulder. "Why do you have two men tattooed on your arm?" I said.

"An old Cayuga tattooed them there. When I was drunk." McBride pushed past me to the fire. "The Cayuga said I was the chosen one, because I have warring blood inside me. He said, 'Only you can free the fighting Indian and white man.' "

McBride gave a harsh laugh and pulled off his wet bandanna. A mass of scars covered his forehead. He breathed in steam that rose from the kettle in which my mother's broth was simmering.

My mother's eyes, full of questions, met mine.

McBride leaned toward the fire. "I have heard about you and your friend's journey to Carantouan. Did you find the skull?" McBride asked, staring at flames.

"Yes," I answered, unable to believe where this was leading me. Not wanting to believe. "You're Big Nose? Daniel's Big Nose? The one who told the story about a giant water creature?" I hoped this trader who'd promised much and given little would say no.

"Perhaps I am."

"But Daniel said Big Nose was an American trader."

"Perhaps I was." He laughed again.

My mother ladled broth, then gestured that McBride sit down. Wikbi flew to his perch on my father's musket. My Brown Bess stood where I had propped her—next to our window. McBride had sold me this gun. He'd said I would do great things with it. But I'd killed my father's beaver for ammunition to feed her.

I sat on the floor beside him. "Who *are* you?" I asked.

At first I thought he hadn't heard me, for he kept his silence, staring at the fire. Then he sat back. In a voice softened now and strangely changed, he said, "I had two mothers. Both are dead. The first had pale skin. She wore a cross like yours." His gaze swept across my mother, who tapped tobacco into a white clay pipe for him to smoke.

"Her cross pressed against my cheek as she tried to save me from attacking Mohawks," he went on. "She fell and there was fire. It burned my forehead. And then my hands. The pain made me pass out. I remembered nothing of the journey to the Mohawks' village—only that I awakened in the soothing arms of She Who Walks on Air.

157

"This second mother had hair like yours, only coarser." McBride's eyes took in the graceful sweep of my mother's hair. It reminded me of folded wings, the way it was pulled back and rolled. "I grew to love this mother as only a son can do. And then white men, American settlers, discovered the village in which I lived. While rescuing me from what they called 'captivity,' they shot her."

McBride turned to me. "Indians killed my first mother when I was six. White men shot my second mother when I was a boy your age. Who am I?"

He stared at his scarred hands. "I hate the Indian. I hate the white man. And yet each is part of me.

"They're always warring. Never do they smoke in peace!" He slammed his fist against the floor. Wikbi squawked. Nohkoomi moaned. He lowered his voice: "Tell me. Did you climb Carantouan? Did you and Daniel free these men?"

I wasn't certain of which men he was speaking. Those inside him? Or those held captive by the locust tree? I wanted to have freed them all. "We didn't free any men. But Daniel and I—"

I was about to tell him of a skull warming to our hands, of a journey almost ended. But the dark look that came over McBride's eyes stopped me: his look was like the grave.

"Bah!" My mother spat at the fire. "My son has told me your story about Carantouan. You should have climbed the sacred hill yourself. Old, dead roots. Fighting men. A river turning red. You want to cause

158

trouble between people—that is all." The troubled expression in my mother's eyes belied the sharpness of her words. McBride's story of dying mothers and fighting men disturbed her.

The trader stood, brushing dried mud off his shirt. To me, he said, "Your cousin Flying Wolf rides with the British. You would be wise to do the same. Flying Wolf has more silver armbands than I can count. His powder horn is never empty."

"You are a two-faced man." My mother's hands trembled as she clenched the white clay pipe. "You lure boys onto forbidden land with the hope that they will end all war. And then you recruit my son to fight it."

He smiled. "The Mohawks call me He Who Runs with the Wind, because they're never certain from which direction I'll come. But you can call me McBride. I'm your trader." He wrapped his red bandanna back around his forehead.

At the door, he said to me, "It's too late to climb Carantouan anyway. Too late to stop this war. I've met Mohawks at Unadilla who torch settlers' cabins along the Susquehanna's northern reaches. Some Mohawks plan to infiltrate the Wyoming Valley. They stalk settlers south of here right now."

I waited for the dark of night to hide me. Then, unseen by Bitter Weed and Bad Shoes, I canoed downriver to make certain Daniel was all right. And to warn him about the Mohawks and McBride. The rain had stopped. Moonlight silvered the Susquehanna. Wikbi perched, a silent sentinel, on my bow. The carved crow nestled in my hunting bag. I wanted to give it to my friend.

I didn't like the way Daniel's moonlit cabin stood alone against the hill. Nor did I like the coldness of the wind that blew around it. It made me fear that Mohawks had already come.

I crept uphill and around the room Daniel's uncle had added. Hiding behind a maple, I cupped my hands and cawed at Daniel's window. The square panes of glass, like water, captured moonlight. Silence answered me. I tried again.

I cawed a third time. Then a fourth. Had Mohawks carried everyone away? But the cabin still was standing. The barn as well. I'd seen drowsy chickens roosting in trees.

Wikbi beat the air around me. Wikbi screeched. A window seemed to shimmer. At first I thought it was a dream, the head that now peeked out. Such unruly hair! I felt like shouting, "Daniel!" I held my hands higher than my shoulders. I extended my right finger, and made the sign for tree. Daniel brought his hands together, saying he would meet me.

We sat in our hollowed sycamore, Daniel's arm against mine. Wikbi sat on my right shoulder and nibbled Daniel's cheek. Although I had more urgent things to say, I'd told Daniel about Crow first: his gift of fire and how this fire had scorched him. I said, "The crow is now my manitou."

"I have a manitou as well. My mother gave it to me." Daniel showed me a silver cross. It was like the one my mother wore, but smaller.

"I've heard the story of this cross," I said. "It's happy and it's sad, like Crow's story. I must tell you of another sadness now. It's about a trader you called Big Nose, who shared with you a dream."

When I was finished with my tale, Daniel replied, "Big Nose can't be McBride. Big Nose believed in freedom and in General Washington. He said power blazed in General Washington's eyes like fire."

"He said the same about the British king. And that I should join the king's forces the way my cousin has. That Flying Wolf's powder horn is always full."

Daniel stared at me. "Big Nose gave me the water creature's tooth. He said he wanted to stop all war. He's a traitor. He lies to us both."

"Yes. But sometimes I think this man speaks true. He sent us to the Chemung River. We found the skull. If the Cayugas hadn't come—"

"We would have seen the locust," Daniel said. "If only we had seen it! Coshmoo. Someone's been slaughtering our cattle. Three nights ago, my uncle found the bloodied heads of two cows propped against our door. He claims Indians did it."

"Mohawks," I whispered. I told him what McBride had said. "Your uncle's militia must be on guard."

"His militia is gone. All the militias are gone. They fight alongside General Washington."

"But Mohawks, Tories, even Cayugas could be slaughtering your cattle! They may take more!"

"I know." Daniel sighed. "The woods are full of shadows. In winter, my uncle discovered two Indians camped in an old hunting cabin near us. I wanted to talk to them. Find out who they were and why they were here. My uncle wouldn't give me a chance. He just shot them."

"You should have stopped him!"

"I tried." Daniel raised his shirt sleeve.

When I saw the angry welts on his arms, I gave Daniel the carved crow. "It's a brave bird," I told him. "It flies high above the trees. It sees beyond the shadows that a man can cast. A crow will bring you courage. My friend. It saddens me to think your uncle beats you."

Daniel fingered the outstretched wings then blurted out, "I wish I could open my cabin door and see the smoke from your village. I wish that we could meet as we always have. I don't like the miles that come between us now." He turned to face me, his eyes on mine. "We must try to meet here every moon."

I kept my eyes on his. A promise.

"Do you still dream of bear?" he asked, glancing at the one I'd drawn in the winter.

"It still gnaws the edges of my sleep. Sometimes I feel as if this bear has walked inside me." I felt great sorrow as I said this, for I knew it to be true.

"This will bring *you* courage." Daniel took off the cross he wore around his neck. He gave this symbol of his manitou to me.

CHAPTER
24

During the month of sprouting corn, wandering Tories, American deserters, Mohawk scouts, and a group of battle-scarred Oneidas passed through our village at Tioga. We kept our cabins open to them all. The Cayugas across the river did the same. But Kschilaan's warriors as well as ours kept sharpened hatchets by their beds.

The Mohawks told us, "The American rebels have cursed the Iroquois! They've sent a black sickness that has devoured ninety lives at Onondaga. The great Six Nations can no longer meet. And now American conjurers bewitch the air. It brings bad dreams and aching bellies. Soon the American rebels will line the Great Warrior's Path with all our bodies."

But the five Oneidas blamed the sickness at Onondaga on the British. They said British conjurers had bewitched the earth. "Our bilberries never ripened," these Oneidas told us. "The squash we planted withered and died. The corn won't grow. The British want us all to die."

No sickness stalked my neutral village, and the corn thrived. My mother said this was a good omen. Still, our women made children play within their sight, and the men didn't venture far. Too many omens traveled through Tioga. We didn't know who or what to believe. Troubled, I found it hard to sleep or eat. The morning following the full moon came, and I canoed downriver to keep a promise.

I waited at the sycamore, but Daniel didn't come. I wondered if he'd heard about the sickness at Onondaga, and about conjurers who'd bewitched the earth and sky. I drew a balled fist, wanting this sign, like a carved crow, to give Daniel courage. I touched the cross I carried in my medicine pouch. An uneasy Wikbi stroked my cheek.

The corn had tassled the day a messenger from my uncle brought the news that ushered war into my valley. "The Senecas have attended a great council held by Colonel Butler at Irondequoit," he said. "As a nation, the Senecas have decided to join the king and take up the hatchet against the American rebels.

"The king has given your Seneca uncles fine weapons, clothes, ostrich feathers, beads, and jingling bells. Within the moon, they will arrive at Tioga Point to celebrate this with you. Your trader, McBride, is with them. He no longer leads a mule train, but rides a prancing stallion—a buckskin."

I didn't want to see McBride. And I dreaded seeing Flying Wolf. Not only because he might be courting White Fawn, but because of Daniel. I feared even more for his safety now.

That night I cawed outside his cabin. Someone stirred in the added room. I slipped away, hoping Daniel had heard and would know to meet me at our sycamore. I waited there, long moments. Finally he came, looking as anxious as I felt.

"We must speak quickly. My family doesn't sleep well. They might awaken and find me gone," he said. "We've heard the Senecas have joined the British. And someone's been killing off our cattle again.

"Three more heads, Coshmoo. Three bloodied heads, three nights: one set against our door, the next against my uncle's shed, the third against the barn. I can't sleep. Yesterday, at dawn, I saw a stocky Indian with heavy, muscled arms, moving through our trees. I've seen this man before. At your harvest feast. He was shooting at targets with his warrior's bow."

"Bitter Weed!" I gasped. "But no. He wouldn't do such a thing. My mother has forbidden it. It must be a Tory. Or a Mohawk. Daniel, they swarm through Tioga Point like fleas."

"We have only one cow left," Daniel said. "We need its milk. My father needs it. He grows weaker."

"He's been cursed," I said, signing my sorrow for this. "My friend. We all are cursed. Sickness devours Iroquois lives. The Oneidas' corn and squash won't grow. Flying Wolf soon arrives at my village. With McBride."

"I hate him. I hate them all. I never know who to

165

trust anymore. Who to believe." Daniel's troubled gaze met mine. "Will you open your cabins to these Senecas again? They've declared war against my people."

"We have no choice. They are our cousins. Flying Wolf's mother and mine are sisters. But Daniel, we keep our cabins open to you as well."

He nodded, but I could tell he was upset. His foot kept scuffling through dead leaves.

"I hate Flying Wolf!" I told him. "I'd send him out to sleep with dogs, but I have no say. Neither do I with McBride. He is our trader."

"A man named Big Nose once told me that all bones are connected. The giant water creature's, yours, mine. He said if we freed the fighting Indian and white man, bones would rise and sing. Coshmoo. These men never will be free!" Daniel stared at the moon-struck branches that rose above us. "Give this to McBride for me."

What he placed in my hand felt cold and silent, like the dead. I held it up in moonlight. "A molar?"

"From a slaughtered cow," he said.

The morning my cousins and McBride arrived, I'd returned from hunting, the doe I'd shot with bow and arrow warm against my back. Gickokwita, a fiery red, rose above the confusion of horses and people milling in the clearing where we held our bonfires. Several men called out to me. I called greetings back as I made my way over to my mother's drying rack. All around, excited Senecas spoke of Irondequoit, Colonel Butler, and his generosity. Like brightly colored butterflies, women wearing new clothes and large, white feathers fluttered here and there, greeting old friends.

Flying Wolf's mother stood beside mine. My aunt twirled back and forth, showing off her new blue skirt. My mother pretended to admire it. I knew she was upset. This bounty would lead to war. I thought the skirt made my aunt look fat.

"Have you ever seen a sword like this?" a voice behind me said. I turned. It was McBride. The buckskin he rode sidled as he withdrew the sword. Sunlight burned off a long curved blade.

"I saw one like that," I said. "In a vision. But my sword was larger and brighter than yours. It seemed more powerful."

McBride laughed. His horse's ears twitched uneasily. "Things are always grander in visions. But you can't take visions from a scabbard. You can't cut throats with them. Visions don't feed empty bellies. They don't keep us clothed."

I couldn't help but admire what he was wearing: a rare white deerskin shirt and leggings, and a silver gorget, shaped like a half-moon, hanging from his neck. But I could not admire his eyes. Oh, his eyes had that look of the grave in them! I turned away.

"Colonel Butler plans to have his army here next spring. He'll bring clothes and swords and ammunition. If you join his army, he'll feed you well." McBride laughed again. I caught the scent of white man's whiskey on his breath.

"Colonel Butler brings a British army to Tioga

Point?" I asked, forcing myself to look at McBride. But only at the stubble on his chin.

"The largest army you've ever seen." He pivoted his horse, leaving me alarmed. This man had left all hope of ending war behind. He wove his fine buckskin in and out of people, over to my cousin's horse.

Flying Wolf, his silver armbands jangling, wheeled his stallion in front of an admiring group of girls. Eagle feathers fluttered from the stallion's mane. A cascade of colored ribbons covered his black withers.

White Fawn and Laughing Water peeked out from among the girls. White Fawn's hair shone blue in the sunlight. She gazed wistfully at the ribbons draped across a stallion that nosed McBride's sweated buckskin as if they were old friends. I felt poor, standing in my moccasins.

Girls squealed as Flying Wolf held up a handful of ribbons. Red, blue, and yellow ribbons fluttered through the air into their eager outstretched hands. Now he reached into a leather sack and brought out a folded square of gold cloth. With his rattlesnake-tattoed hand, my cousin tossed the cloth to White Fawn.

White Fawn, eyes glittering, caught it.

I kept my face like stone, not wanting anyone to sense the anger I was feeling. My cousin had no right to give White Fawn such a gift. White Fawn should not have accepted it. Flying Wolf's mother might begin marriage talk with White Fawn's. I would climb Carantouan alone and brave a hundred thundering spirits to keep my cousin from marrying a girl who'd stood small beneath tall trees and netted shad with me. That night, I sat with Wikbi beside my river and we schemed.

The next morning, I left a cabin filled with the sounds of sleeping. Wikbi and Nohkoomi were gone—probably out hunting. I kept to the fog-shrouded woods surrounding the village. I wanted no one to see me, for they would ask, "Why do you slink through the woods at this hour? What do you have hidden in your arms? A deer's heart and liver?" With sly looks, they would say, "Coshmoo. These are the best parts of the deer! Who are they for?"

Three girls were already out, singing softly as they gathered wood for cooking fires. I avoided them, staying among the misted trees. The ground sloped gently. Brush that had been cleared from the cattle pasture was piled to the side of a narrow path leading to the river. I pulled back a large fir branch and crept into the pile. I replaced the limb and, concealed by arching branches, crouched and waited. Through a small opening, I could see the section of river where White Fawn always came to fetch the morning's water.

Moments passed. Tiny bugs swarmed within the golden feathers that warmed my hiding place. As Gickokwita shed his sleep, I thought about McBride. The cow's tooth would be a fitting gift for him. He spoke laughingly of an army that would gather in Carantouan's shadow. The dream in him had died.

The village was awakening. My heart began to beat in time to the pounding of corn in mortars. Soon someone would pass by. I asked the Great Creator to make that someone White Fawn.

My heartbeat quickened at the sound of footsteps. I backed deeper into the brush. To my right, through a tangle of branches, I saw a patch of red approaching. Was it Laughing Water? Red Wing?

I saw the fullness of a red cloth skirt and a pair of deerskin leggings. It could be any one of several girls. I held my breath. The skirt and leggings paused. A soft, low voice began a song of thanks to Gickokwita for his warming light. I let my breath out slowly. I knew this voice. The song of thanks continued. Quilled moccasins and two wooden buckets added to its beauty, swinging past in a quick and easy movement.

I breathed a prayer of thanks to the Great Creator, then pulled back the fir branch. I crawled out and whispered, "White Fawn."

She gasped, facing me with large dark eyes.

"We must talk." I grabbed her arm before she could try to flee.

"Coshmoo . . ." Anxiously, she glanced over her shoulder. Wisps of smoke rose above the stand of trees that shielded us from village eyes.

"No one comes," I said. "You talked to me before, when I showed you a small carved crow. Look, what I have brought you now." I felt her watching me as I opened the gifts I had wrapped in grass.

"A deer's heart and liver. They're given with my mother's blessing," I said, even though my mother didn't know what I was doing. She'd said I wasn't old enough to give presents to a woman. By the time I was, I wouldn't have to give them, for I'd be a powerful chief who spoke for peace. Women would flock to me.

"My mother will thank yours," White Fawn said. She set her buckets on the ground and I handed her the gifts. For a moment, our fingers touched. I felt sudden heat, as if something powerful had passed between us. A flow of black hair covered White Fawn's face when she placed the heart and liver in one of her buckets.

"You accepted Flying Wolf's cloth," I said.

"Another would have caught it if I hadn't. The cloth feels like river water, cool and light." She raised her head. Her cheeks were flushed, her eyes full of feeling. I wished I knew for whom.

Fog rose off the Susquehanna. The way the sun glanced off the water reminded me of the diamond pattern on a rattler's back and the snake that slithered through my scheme. I said, "Do you remember when you cooked shad roe for Elk Hair and me?"

"The shad roe popped and we shared dreams."

"You had dreamt about a husband who turned into a timber rattler."

"I turned my moccasins over every night, so that this man who was a snake would never marry me."

"It's easy for moccasins to be tipped over. Easy to have dreams we don't recall. Have you seen my cousin's new tattoo?"

"The timber rattler? You want me to believe that Flying Wolf was the husband in my dream?" She laughed when I nodded. Smiling to herself, she picked up her buckets and with a saucy step walked down the path leading to the river. She made all fears and schemes seem foolish.

CHAPTER
25

———◆———

A voice was crying through the night woods: "We-ko-lis. We-ko-lis." A small bird with rounded wings darted through the leafy trees, repeating the cry. It echoed through the eastern hills over which my Elder Brother Moon was rising.

The lonely sound made me feel empty. Perhaps if White Fawn's hands had not touched mine . . . Perhaps if we hadn't talked, I wouldn't have felt this way. I longed for her presence beside me on this rocky spit that jutted out into the Susquehanna. I wanted to see Daniel, too. McBride had changed and he worried me with his fine clothes and his talk of Colonel Butler's army.

Wikbi cooed. He danced along my shoulder, then pressed his wing against my cheek. I was grateful for his company. I dug my finger into the short feathers behind his eyes and gently rubbed the itchy spot he couldn't reach. The wind blew off the land, bringing the scent of burning hickory and the murmur of voices.

Soon I'd have to join the others for a night of feast and dancing. Even the Cayugas from across the river had come. But for now, I was grateful for a secluded spot in which to think.

The full moon rose over the Susquehanna. I threw a stone into the moon's reflection; the water rippled, making ever-widening circles. Perhaps Flying Wolf and McBride soon will leave, I told myself. Then everything will go back to the way it used to be. There'll be no omens, no talk of war. Come spring, I'll fish again with White Fawn.

I knew this was only a dream, but I liked getting lost in it. I pictured myself with White Fawn and Elk Hair. We netted shad from my canoe. The Susquehanna reflected happy faces. Wikbi pranced among the fish we'd caught, and White Fawn told her stories.

"We-ko-lis." The lonely cry echoed through my dream. It awakened me from sunlight to a deepening night. The wind carried the sound of rising voices. Wikbi fluffed his feathers, his dark eyes open and alert. I stared where he was staring. The moon, reflected in the water, had gathered shadows.

I'd never seen anything like it before. A rearing horse with bared teeth, flattened ears, and threatening hooves appeared to darken the moon's eastern curve. I threw a stone at the reflection, hoping the vision would disappear. The ripples widened. The image darkened.

Thinking my river played games with me, I stared at the moon itself. I watched the dark shape of the horse advance. I saw muscled shoulders and a wind-whipped mane. I began to feel the way I had on my vision quest—light-headed, queasy, and afraid. I ran my hand along Wikbi's head and wings. His beak opened, then shut without a sound.

Behind me, village dogs began to howl, their voices pitched in fear. I knew I should return to the village, but the awful vision in the moon held me.

"Coshmoo!" Elk Hair came running through laurel and down the shallow bank. Wikbi lifted off my shoulder. Silently, he swooped, then landed on a large rock within my seeing but beyond reach. I rose to my feet.

"I've been searching for you. Look. The moon." Elk Hair pointed to the sky.

It was then I knew that this vision in the moon was not mine alone. Others saw it, too. Did Daniel? Did it frighten him? The moon's western curve had begun to dim.

"Your mother asked me to find you," Elk Hair said. "Quickly. We must return to the village. Everyone is outside. Everyone is talking about this moon."

Wikbi dipped and zigzagged, disappearing into darkness overhead. Near White Fawn's hut, the small, sturdy figure of Elk Hair's younger brother Much Talk raced down a beaten path toward us. "Bitter Weed says a great war is about to be raged on the face of the moon!" he said.

The muscled shapes of two rearing horses approached each other now, one coming from the moon's

174

eastern rim, the other, a smaller one, advancing from the west. Dogs howled. My heart beat loudly like a drum.

"Bitter Weed has already lit the bonfire. Come!" Much Talk grabbed my hand and pulled me toward the fire that blazed within the clearing. People were gathering around it. Flames licked the sky like the tongues of the two dogs, now loping, now snapping at each other as we hurried by.

McBride stood beside my cousin. McBride's glazed eyes stared at mine. Reflecting fire, his eyes burned red. I thought, This man's been drinking. *He should not be here.* The trader turned to Flying Wolf and pointed to the moon. The eastern horse was growing larger, feeding off the advancing shadow of the western one.

"Elk Hair. You found my son." My mother fingered her cross. Behind her anxious women moaned.

"He was crouched by the river. Dreaming."

"Without such dreams, we would be like the shad, swimming upstream only to die within a fishnet." Her surprising words and the sight of her, small against the darkening moon, worried me.

Broken Stone brushed past. The bearskin cap, robe, leggings, and wooden mask he wore had transformed him into Meesing—the great and powerful masked being who protects us all. Meesing balanced a fat buck on his furred shoulder.

"The spirits are angry." Meesing placed the buck at my mother's moccasined feet. "We must appease them."

She nodded, gazing at the raging horses. The eastern horse had almost overtaken the western one. Now there was one large head, one set of forelegs, and . . . two hindquarters. With a knife, Meesing started hacking off the buck's flank.

I glanced away, searching for the easy coolness of water curling through the night. I saw White Fawn. She carried a small, crying child. White Fawn glanced at me. Her large eyes looked frightened.

Don't be afraid, I thought. I willed my words to enter her heart as much as I willed them to enter mine. She ducked her head to comfort the child, then walked on.

Meesing threw the buck's flank into the bonfire. "Elder Brother," he cried, addressing the moon, "your people here are fearful! Take pity on them now! Your children whimper. Your women cry. Accept this sacrifice they bring! May they find favor in your sight."

Meesing shook his dried tortoiseshell. "Brother Wind! Carry the smoke of burning flesh. Whisper its essence into our Elder Brother's ear. Beseech him to clear his face of these two dark horses, these omens we do not understand."

Meesing howled. In feet covered by bear claws, he danced, hitching forward and then back, a dark furred shape circling a fire that carried the scent of scorched flesh into the sky. Standing in a circle, everybody watched him. We listened to the beat of dried beans in a tortoiseshell. Suddenly, within this beat, McBride's drunken voice cried out:

"This darkened moon bodes ill! Don't you see? The hungry-mouthed Americans form the black horse from the east that devours you!"

Dried beans answered the British trader. Beans shaken in a shell to the beat of frightened hearts. At my side, my mother raised her arms. Draped in a red cloth shawl, they reminded me of wings. She said, "This white man should not have spoken! He should not give meaning to so powerful an omen!"

But I wanted to give voice to this omen, too. For its meaning became clear to me. These dark horses were not Americans devouring us. They were Americans battling the British. The war of these two dark horses threatened to destroy everything, including the moon. I needed to speak, but angry, frightened voices rose like some great furred monster, overpowering the rhythmic shaking of the tortoiseshell. Hands pointed to the sky.

Someone howled, "The Americans form the black horse that devours all."

McBride shouted, "Senecas, Cayugas, Delawares—all must unite. Raise your tomahawks of war! Kill the American rebels who steal not only your rivers and your land, but your moon as well."

"McBride!" As if outside myself, I heard my voice shriek out his name. Wanting to silence him. Daniel was American. Daniel was my friend. I could never raise a tomahawk against him.

But some dark power had already been unleashed. I heard it in Flying Wolf's answering howl, now echoed by Cayugas and by *Bitter Weed*. I saw it in

Bitter Weed's tomahawk, now flung and embedded in our painted post. Our warriors echoed Bitter Weed's rage. What was happening to us?

McBride's strange eyes fixed on mine. His thin-lipped mouth opened—a shallow, toothy cave. He shrieked. Like bats, his eerie howls flew upward. I saw the bats turn into buzzards. A flock of buzzards feeding on a field of bones. I saw feathers caught in barbed wire. A clay pipe resting on a heap of cold, dead bones. It was the frightening vision I'd once seen in my father's eyes.

"Coshmoo." My mother's arm brushed mine. Meesing, in a slow dance, continued to circle the fire. "Join Meesing, and the others will follow. We must not talk of war. We must appease the spirits."

I began to dance, hitching my feet, forward and then back. One by one, the other warriors joined me in a long line behind Meesing. I felt McBride's dancing shadow at my back. I willed my fearful, aching heart to beat in time to the rattle of the tortoiseshell.

Within the smell of burning flesh, within the howls of men and boys, I danced while the rearing stallion from the east completely devoured the stallion from the west. As its darkness overtook our Elder Brother, the women sang, beseeching the moon to protect us from any danger its blackened face foretold. My mother's voice wove a spell around the rest—this low-pitched melodic voice that had lulled me to sleep when I was small; this voice that since my father's death the village elders had listened to, obeyed.

I felt the heartbeat of my people echoed in my mother's voice. I sensed all their hope and fear and sorrow. The night grew deeper still. My mother wailed. She raised her arms, her clenched hands seeming to defy the sky. I recalled hands like these, recalled, as if I'd seen it myself, the snow-covered body of my father sprawled on the crest of Carantouan. And I wondered, Among the swirling mists that gathered there, how many fearful visions had my father seen?

CHAPTER 26

———

Bitter Weed held the dried liver over a small bowl filled with water. Spotted Owl, Bad Shoes, Broken Stone, and I watched him. It was the morning after the Moon of Two Dark Horses, and Bitter Weed said, "If blood from the deer's liver circles before sinking, the moon will recover. If it doesn't circle, our moon will die."

We sang for the blood to circle, but it sank.

Later, the moon rose untroubled over distant hills, but we knew that inside, where we couldn't see, our moon had been cursed. Broken Stone donned the robe and mask that transformed him into Meesing. For the next seven nights, we held sacrificial feasts and dances, beseeching the Great Creator to take pity, to free our troubled moon and us from darkness. Hate, fired by McBride, ran high. Beyond my mother's hearing, he reminded our warriors of Teedyuscung's death. The loss of land. The lack of ammunition. The American settlers who'd cursed us.

For six of the seven nights of sacrifice, the bear with the hunger of a thousand winters nosed the door-flaps of my sleep. On the seventh night, the bear scraped his claws against my door. A moment later, with only the length of my musket between us, I stared into his hungry eyes. I didn't hesitate this time. I fired. The bear exploded into a thousand stars. To my horror, these stars drew together. They formed another bear, larger than the first—a silver bear with eyes like embers. The porch steps sagged beneath his feet.

I shot this bear. He exploded into a thousand suns, lighting up the night. These suns drew together. They formed a golden bear whose feet were too large to climb steps. His claws ripped off our roof. I aimed my musket at the fierce head glaring down at me. I fired and the third bear exploded into a thousand raging fires.

I shot as hot flames licked the sky. I shot as fiery claws ripped the night. I shot at teeth tearing through the moon and stars. Over and over, I fired my musket, my heart pounding. And in the middle of my loud and frantic firing, a word exploded in my head. A word shouted so loudly it frightened away the flaming bear and drowned out the roar of musket fire.

"Coshmoo!" It was Daniel's voice.

I awakened, covered in cold sweat. Flames flickered in the fireplace. Beneath my father's musket, my crow and my mother's dog were wide awake and staring at me.

I drew on my moccasins, grabbed my musket,

181

powder horn, and bullet pouch, then ducked outside. Wikbi, my faithful crow, flew with me through the hot, damp night.

Daniel's cabin stood still and silent, washed by moonlight. I was too anxious to see him to ask myself why no smoke rose from his chimney. It was the first time Daniel had walked within my dreams and called me. Daniel had to be here.

I cupped my hands and cawed, impatient to see a head with unruly hair peek out from a window. No head did. I thought Daniel couldn't hear me. No one stirred in his uncle's room, so I crept closer. I crouched behind the maple where I'd watched chickens scratch for grubs. I wondered where the chickens were. The one cow.

Seven times I cawed to a dark and lifeless window. Seven times I felt hope and then despair. Wikbi must have sensed my growing desperation, for the last three times, his caws joined mine. I told myself, Daniel can't be gone. He'd never leave without telling me. Unless someone who enjoyed cutting heads off cows had attacked him. Or killed him. Or dragged him away.

I leaned against the maple. *Daniel was gone.*

Dawn came. Sunlight made bottles in a window shine: a large green bottle, a honey-colored bottle, a clear glass bottle, and five colored blue like Daniel's eyes. I peered in a window, afraid of what I'd see. A pitcher and three mugs sat neatly on the table. Mrs.

Seibert's black iron kettle hung in the fireplace. Her spider pan sat on the floor. I saw no bodies, no sign of struggle, anywhere.

I ran to the other side of the cabin. That was when I saw the door. Barred and padlocked. I felt such sadness. Such relief.

"If the Seiberts had been attacked, this door would have stood open," I told my mother later. She shelled beans on our porch steps. I was too out of breath, too caught up in thoughts of Daniel to notice her guarded look. "But something's happened to them. If they'd just moved away, they'd have taken their belongings."

"Not if they were frightened. Too many shadows crowd our poor troubled land. You said Daniel spoke to you within a dream?" My mother glanced to her right. The far end of the porch lay in darkness. I could see nothing there.

"Daniel shouted my name. He cried out to me," I said as a shadow now uncurled from that darkness— *McBride.*

"It's a powerful friendship that speaks through dreams," my mother said, watching the trader's slow approach. His unsteady footsteps on our porch sounded hollow. He smelled of white man's whiskey, again. His deerskin shirt was stained.

In a slow, slurred voice he said to me, "You and that American boy are still friends?"

"We are *nitis*, closest friends. We always will be." I challenged the drunken white man, stared at his eyes. For a moment, the dead look within them lifted. His eyes pleaded with me. Made me wish I held a sword. I wanted to free the two men I saw fighting in their dull green depths: a scalp-locked warrior and a white man.

Three nights later, McBride left with my Seneca cousins. Bitter Weed and five of our warriors shaved their heads and joined them. They traveled north to fight alongside Colonel Butler and his Rangers. Neither my mother nor our elders could stop these warriors. It was their choice. But my mother's eyes sang with pain as she took in Bitter Weed's war paint. She whispered to me. "Coshmoo. *You* are my hope. *You* must stand beside me. Together we will keep our peaceful village out of this white man's war."

That fall, I canoed south many times to see if the Seiberts had returned. Someone had gathered their corn and wheat, but it wasn't Daniel. No smoke ever rose from his chimney. I never caught his scent. Our sycamore felt so empty. I left a message for him there, telling him I hoped that wherever he might be, he'd find wondrous bones. Giant bones, and freedom.

The maple leaves turned red and drumbeats everywhere sang of war. Dreams of bear and the Moon of Two Dark Horses stalked me. Beneath angry, blood-red leaves, I began to carve wolves. Seven of them, all within a single piece of walnut. As the first wolf emerged, my mother looked pleased. She said, "You carve Nohkoomi." But as I gave voice to the spirit of this wolf, my mother frowned and said, "Nohkoomi rarely bares her teeth. Nor does she raise her hackles. Who is this wolf?"

"The Senecas," I replied.

The second wolf emerged. The first wolf had its teeth clamped around this smaller, frailer one's neck. My mother asked who this wolf might be. I told her, "The Oneidas." A third wolf, then a fourth came to life within the walnut. Soon, I'd carved six wolves, one for each nation within the Iroquois League. It was hard to tell where one wolf began and one left off. All were locked in combat, trying to destroy each other. A seventh wolf, head lowered, watched narrow-eyed from the side.

"Who is this seventh wolf?" my mother asked.

"The Delawares," I replied.

I didn't carve the bloodied knife that was the white man's war, but it was there.

My mother didn't like the carving. She told me to put it in a dark place, out of sight. That was when she tried to deny the tale she'd once told Flying Wolf and me. "I think the Huron from the north who'd told me the story had seen too many winters. His eyes were clouded. No wolf would attack his wounded brother."

I said, "A hungry wolf has licked the blade. His brother wolves attack him now. Soon, they'll destroy each other. Don't you see? Since the Moon of Two Dark Horses, everyone but the Delawares has taken sides. Drums don't lie! Senecas, Mohawks, Onondagas, and Cayugas fight for the British. The Tuscaroras and Oneidas have joined the American side."

My mother still tried to deny the story. "The Huron was drunk on rum when he told it to me.

Wolves are brothers. They protect, they don't kill each other."

She was denying something we both knew was true. The Six Nations of the Iroquois had fought against and killed each other, first in the white man's battle at Oriskany and later at Saratoga. Several great sachems died. Mourning cries, echoing from one village to another, brought the news.

I turned the soles of my moccasins upward, for in the nightmare of this time, I was afraid a bear would devour my dreams. And in this no-dreaming time, Flying Wolf, three Seneca warriors, and five of our Delawares brought Bitter Weed home, draped across the withers of a weary, sweat-streaked stallion.

"Bitter Weed fought like a warrior," Flying Wolf told my mother. "He would be with us now if an American soldier hadn't run a bayonet through his back. His life is worth five white men's lives."

"Ten," said Spotted Owl, "for the American devil cut off his ears."

My mother wept as we buried Bitter Weed near the apple orchard in which the bones of the Ancient Warrior lay. In spite of all he'd done, Bitter Weed was one of our men. I helped lower him into his grave. The fine deerskin the women had dressed him in covered the bayonet wound. But nothing could hide the bloodied holes on each side of his head.

Flying Wolf, leading the group of five embittered warriors, rode south to avenge Bitter Weed's death. This time, my mother couldn't stop him. Blood must be paid for with blood. I hunted deer with a bow and arrow and saved what ammunition I had to protect my neutral village. I forgot about the fighting men Daniel and I had tried to free. It was a foolish dream. Daniel was gone. The Moon of Two Dark Horses had terrorized the sky. Bitter Weed had been dishonored.

Within the moon, Flying Wolf and the other warriors returned. Giving the death halloo, they galloped through our pastures, scattering the cattle. They brought five prisoners, scalps, and bounty with them. Among this bounty were three kegs of gunpowder and bottles. Beautiful glass bottles looted from a cabin that they'd burned.

CHAPTER 27

The square-shouldered green bottle sat in our window the way it once had sat in Daniel's—gathering light. The squat honey-colored bottle and the clear one with the ribbed design flanked it. The five small blue bottles surrounded them like children. My mother had always loved these bottles. She'd asked Flying Wolf to leave them with us, not as war bounty, but as a reminder of a friendship.

Green, blue, and honey-colored light splashed across Mr. Sutton's dark wool coat. He and a farmer, Mr. Jenkins, had come upriver to see about a friend of theirs who was taken prisoner by an Indian raiding party ten nights earlier. This friend, who'd been captured along with four other men, was a Quaker, like Mr. Sutton. Quakers didn't believe in war.

"Neither do I," my mother said.

"This we've heard." Mr. Sutton fingered his watch chain while, outside on our porch, the warriors who'd escorted him and Mr. Jenkins to our cabin whispered uneasily. I wished Broken Stone were here to calm them. But Broken Stone was hunting.

"Ten nights ago, prisoners stayed in our village. Your Quaker friend was with them," my mother said. "The prisoners were hungry and we gave them food. They were cold. We gave them shelter. Then the Senecas took them north, maybe eight nights past."

"We've been told you know these Senecas well. That you might convince them to release our friend," Mr. Sutton said.

"Who told you this?"

"A farmer's son. He lived downriver at Sheshequin." Mr. Sutton was looking at the bottles shining in our window.

"You've seen the farmer's son? Daniel? Is he well?" I asked.

"He's well," Mr. Jenkins said. "But he's still grieving." At my blank look he continued, "His father died."

"*Daniel's* father died?" I said, not wanting to believe it. Hoping maybe I'd heard wrong. The white man's words were tricksters. Sometimes they danced all over when they should have stood still.

"At my mill," Mr. Sutton said. "It was a hot day, four months ago. The family had stopped to rest on their way downriver to the Wyoming Valley. They hoped to find a doctor there. And some peace. Someone had been killing off their cattle, one by one." The sadness in this Quaker's eyes made me feel guilty. But I hadn't killed these cattle!

189

"The man was weak. He'd been coughing blood," Mr. Sutton said. "He died with his head pillowed on his wife's lap. Frail thing. I felt sorry for her. The small girl couldn't stop crying. And the boy, well, he looked stunned."

"Where is he now?" I asked. "You must have seen him if he spoke to you of Senecas, and of Delawares who will help you."

"Three nights ago, he was at my mill with his uncle. They'd stopped to get rope to repair their raft. They were going upriver to collect the things they'd left in their haste to find a doctor. He could be staying at Sheshequin now."

But there was no place at Sheshequin for Daniel to stay! His cabin had been looted and burned while he was gone. Did Mr. Sutton know this? He kept glancing at our bottles.

He said to my mother, "The boy claimed he and your son, Coshmoo, were friends."

"Closest friends," my mother said. Outside, the restless warriors began to chant. To me, their voices were but chirping birds next to the picture that thundered through my head—Daniel, standing among the burned timbers of his home.

A warrior's fist banged against our door. Just once. My mother's lips tightened to a thin, pale line.

"Could you send a messenger to the Senecas? Ask that they return our friend, along with the others they captured?" Mr. Sutton asked.

My mother shook her head. "All these men, including your Quaker friend, are allied in their hatred for the British king. If I were to intercede for them, others might take it to mean I've joined the Americans. They might take revenge on my people. I wish to live in peace with you, my friends. But I want no Delaware blood shed in your white man's war."

Outside, the warriors' chants grew louder. They wanted to frighten away settlers who thought they could walk freely into our peaceful village as if it were their land. Ever since the Moon of Two Dark Horses, the warriors had been like this. It was hard for my mother to contain them.

An uneasy Mr. Sutton and Mr. Jenkins drank broth by our fire while Gickokwita's dying rays slanted through our window. After dark, my mother and I led them to the Susquehanna. They boarded a canoe my mother gave them and, carrying news of colored bottles and Queen Esther's restless warriors, fled south.

The next day I paddled downriver. I had to tell Daniel I had nothing to do with the burning of his farm. War had done it. The white man's war.

At Sheshequin, I found two sets of footprints leading from the ashes of his cabin to the ashes of a blacksmith's shed to the blackened timbers of a barn. I saw prints in ash where one foot had swept angrily back and forth.

I searched for Daniel along Cash Creek. I ran through woods, and up and down through hollows. I saw no further sign of Daniel until I reached the sycamore. There I caught his scent. Inside our tree, he had drawn a bear. It blackened all the messages we had left.

I traveled downriver many times after that, hoping to see and talk to my friend. Each time I saw the charred remains of Daniel's home, I wanted to rebuild it and fill its emptiness with happy songs. Snow soon covered Daniel's footprints. His scent, which had lingered in the sycamore, slowly faded, then was gone. I wondered where he was. In the Wyoming Valley? Was his frog-faced uncle with him? I wished warm fires for Daniel.

The winter brought more snow than we had ever seen. Fighting armies retreated to their winter camps, and now a different kind of war was fought. For snow piled on top of snow. Then came freezing rain. And always, a bitter wind was blowing.

Our starving cattle huddled near the apple orchard, their backs turned to this biting wind that froze their ears and tails. One by one, our cattle died, taking with them the milk we liked to drink. We ate their meat, boiled the bones and sucked them dry. The hungry days burned like candles, short and quick, giving little light.

No trader, American or British, came near us. But Kschilaan, the Cayuga sachem, visited once. Spies lurked in the snow-covered hills above Tioga, he said. One of his warriors had been killed. A brass button from an American uniform was found clenched in his hand.

Kschilaan said it was becoming too difficult for his

village to stay neutral in the white man's war. His men weren't trusted by either side. Trade goods were scarce. Everyone hungered. Some without blankets had frozen to death. Other Cayugas had joined the British. Kschilaan would, too, and if Colonel Butler's Rangers came to Tioga Point next spring, Kschilaan's warriors would join them. The British king was powerful. And rich.

That winter, my mother saved the choicest cuts of meat for me. "You need strength to stand beside me. We must stand strong. I want no wounded warriors. No mourning wails in my village. I will not let my people fight a white man's war."

I ate the meat. Afraid to dream, I kept my moccasin soles turned upward. Word came by muffled drumbeat that people everywhere were dying. From old wounds. Lack of food. Endless snow. I imagined Daniel, body hunkered against the wind. He warmed his hands by holding them within his armpits. His face was gaunt with hunger and he wore no shoes. Would anyone survive this winter?

On a dark day, I found myself carving crows—two crows within a single piece of walnut. One was Daniel; the other, me. We huddled together like frozen cattle. I placed the carving on the table beneath the window that held the colored bottles.

That night, the wind slammed snow and sleet against the north side of my cabin. Frost lined the inside of the walls. Cold seeped through my bones. I buried myself beneath two blankets and a bearskin.

Wikbi hopped onto my bed and did something he'd never done. He nested in the hollow formed by the back of my neck and head. I welcomed the warmth of Wikbi's unexpected company. I liked the way he preened my hair, tugging it gently, strand by strand.

CHAPTER
28

In a lull between two snowstorms, the Delaware messenger came. Weary and frostbitten, he brought us disturbing news that had traveled with him from the far side of the Alleghenies. An American militia, for no reason anyone could understand, had shot at and plundered friendly Delaware camps along the Shenango River. Soon after, the same militia attacked four Delaware women and a boy who'd been making salt near Mahoning Creek. The boy and three of the women had died. The other woman was taken captive. Neutral Delawares everywhere were outraged.

"Four women and a boy! They were chipping salt with broken hatchets! That is all!" my mother told our elders. "If Americans attacked these innocent ones who live on the far side of the Alleghenies, I fear what they might do to us, who live at Tioga, the gateway to their land."

"We will keep our war hatchets sharpened," Broken Stone replied. "And loaded muskets by our beds."

195

When we were alone, my mother reached over my head and took down the carving of the wolves I'd done earlier. Tears filled her eyes as she ran her hands over each one. "The seventh wolf still watches. My son. How much more can we allow to happen before the seventh wolf joins in?"

That winter, we stayed close to Tioga Point and took what furs we could from the wildcat, raccoon, otter, and fox that roamed the woods bordering the village. We needed ammunition more than ever now. How else could we protect our peaceful homes? The women didn't venture to their sugar camp on the far side of the hills. They tapped what sap they could from nearby maples. It snowed too much!

Wikbi slept with me each night. Nohkoomi rarely left my mother's side. One day, I came upon my mother in the apple orchard. Head bowed, she prayed beside the Ancient Warrior's grave. A chilly wind brought several of her words to me: Teedyuscung; a homeland, lost; the bear.

That night, as I was sleeping, Nohkoomi knocked over my moccasins. I dreamt. Daniel and I were crows, and there was a place we had to go—a distant lodge. Inside lived a powerful water creature to whom we had to speak before it was too late. A bad storm was rising.

Thunder Beings rumbled as we flew toward a distant light. Their fiery arrows scorched our feathers. We wanted to turn back. Voices kept calling, "Don't give up!" So we flew on. But we were small. And the wounded sky so big.

I awakened the next morning feeling as if all hope had fled. Wikbi chirred. He nestled against my neck as if to say, "Everything will be all right." Nohkoomi snored, her nose resting on my moccasins.

It snowed well into the spring. Rumors said the bitter weather had claimed the lives of many Americans living east of the Allegheny Mountains. Lined up, their frozen corpses would stretch from Tioga to the sea. Rumors said that General Washington had died. On the backs of these rumors rode Colonel Butler's army. Four hundred white men and almost twice as many Cayugas and Senecas were descending on Tioga Point. McBride and Flying Wolf rode with them.

Colonel Butler's army arrived just as Gickokwita cleared the eastern hills. The army set up camp across the river. It was after the shadbush had bloomed, I remember. Heat had replaced the numbing cold. Lowanachen, the north wind, brought the sound of soldiers marching and the uncommon scent of British cooking fires. My mother sorted seeds for planting. That summer she hoped to harvest corn and squash and beans.

Since the night I'd dreamt of crows, I kept my moccasins turned upward, hoping beyond hope to complete a journey. I didn't dream of Daniel again, but I sensed his presence everywhere. When a warm spell thawed the frozen Susquehanna, I heard his name in the crack of heaving ice. When the piercing blue of sky puddled in the melting snow, I saw Daniel's eyes. His hair was Wikbi's jumbled nest. His smile the happy dip of goldfinch wings. I thought, Daniel can't be in the Wyoming Valley, because he feels so near.

I should have acted on this feeling. I should have searched for Daniel in the hollowed sycamore. Along the Chemung's banks. On Carantouan itself. The sacred hill would have spoken. This I know. Carantouan would have said, "Look deep within my hollow and you will find your friend." Then I could have found him before McBride and Flying Wolf did.

"He's been spying on Cayugas. And on your people, too!" Flying Wolf said, as McBride thrust Daniel before my mother and our elders. It was late afternoon. The seeds my mother had sorted for planting were heaped in three baskets next to Daniel's feet. His shoes were cracked and broken. Outside our cabin, people were gathering. They'd heard that a spy had been caught.

Daniel's face was red and chapped, the left cheek gashed. He stared at our packed-earth floor. A part of me cried out to him, "Look up. Draw strength from me." The other part screamed, *"What are you doing here?"*

"Daniel has always been free to visit us," my mother told Flying Wolf. "What makes you think that he was spying?"

"This!" Flying Wolf waved a white man's paper in front of my mother's face. "He was about to take *this* downriver when we caught him."

I saw drawings on the paper, two lines meeting to form an arrowhead—Tioga Point! I saw stick men.

Muskets. British flags raised above what looked like two villages—the Cayugas' and mine. All I could think was: The picture's wrong. No flag, British or American, hovers over us.

"It shows Americans how to attack the softness of our underbelly. Look! It reveals secret paths and places where our defenses are weak!" Flying Wolf pointed to snaking lines and dark marks that looked like rocks. "It tells Americans how many warriors Queen Esther has!"

His words hung like smoke in the air. Outside, angry voices buzzed against our window. Daniel raised his head.

Flying Wolf gave the paper to my mother. Her hands trembled. I thought, This can't be true. Daniel wouldn't betray my people. He stared at his mother's bottles lined up on our windowsill. This made me feel sick inside. *Would he?*

"Our scouting party rode by the lair the boy and three men had made within the hollow formed by an uprooted locust," McBride said as the paper now was passed from hand to hand. "They tried to ambush us. One was the blacksmith. I'd never seen the other two. We shot them.

"Queerest thing—the boy didn't run. He knelt among the roots and wailed." An odd expression, like a candle passing before a window, crossed McBride's green eyes.

Daniel looked at me. I understood the sorrow in his eyes. But *I* hadn't stolen the bottles or burned his cabin. My people hadn't joined the British. I'd done nothing to harm him. And now he'd betrayed my people. Me.

"It's good we were scouting for Colonel Butler. Good I caught the boy. He would have taken this," McBride waved the paper, "to Americans living in the Wyoming Valley."

"Americans everywhere betray the Delawares," Flying Wolf said softly, looking from one man to the other. "They kill Delaware women and children. They betray old friends."

I wanted to be angry with Daniel, but I couldn't. He was so thin! His pants were torn and bloodstained, his right leg wounded.

"Why have you brought the boy to me?" my mother asked McBride. "You could have taken him to Kschilaan. After all, you found him on Cayuga land."

He shrugged, that queer candlelit expression still within his eyes. Flying Wolf grinned. Outside, restless moccasins padded up and down our porch. Someone yelled, "There's been too much talk. The white boy was spying. Let him run for his life." *The gauntlet.*

Daniel's eyes searched mine. There was nothing I could do to help him. Whenever prisoners were taken, they had to face the gauntlet.

"Perhaps now, the Delawares will join Colonel Butler's army," Flying Wolf said. "Along with their Seneca and Cayuga cousins, they'll build canoes and rafts. And then, when the nights are long and hot, we'll all slip quietly downriver past Sheshequin, Towanda, and Wyalusing to . . . the valley."

Daniel flinched. And I couldn't help myself. I saw his mother and his sister. Saw this force of canoes and rafts through Daniel's eyes. Like ants, they swarmed down the winding river. They devoured everything along its banks—men, women, children, cabins, apple trees. As they entered the valley, the hungry ants drew together like a cloud. They formed two ears. A probing nose. Raking claws. Two eyes.

CHAPTER 29

———

I stood beside Daniel at the bend in the narrow meadow where, in spring, my people held races to celebrate the shad. Broken Stone stood behind him. McBride held on to Daniel's arm.

People holding axes, clubs, branches, hoes, and hatchets jostled one another as they formed the two lines Daniel was to run between. I told myself: If Daniel ignores the pain in his wounded leg and runs swiftly, he'll avoid most of the blows. He'll show my people how brave he is. He'll survive their punishment. His run, from the meadow's bend to the painted post, is only fifty paces.

Bad Shoes was sharpening his hatchet near us. Daniel stiffened.

"He won't hit you with the edge of the blade. No one will. As long as you run. Whatever you do, don't stop. Be brave like your General Washington," I told him.

"General Washington is dead." Daniel's chapped

face had turned as white as bone. So he'd heard the rumor, too.

"Lean on the spirit of the crow I carved for you," I whispered.

"My uncle burned it." Daniel stared at the ground.

Flying Wolf hallooed. He stood near the painted post, brandishing his axe. Bad Shoes, Spotted Owl, and Red Hawk all picked up his cry.

From my medicine pouch, I withdrew the cross Daniel once had given me. I hung this cross around his neck and forced two of Wikbi's feathers into his hand.

"Coshmoo." My mother reached out and touched my arm. For the first time I could remember, her golden eyes looked dazed. I walked away. Leaving her. Leaving Daniel. McBride's footsteps tailed me.

I stood beside Elk Hair, five paces from the painted post. McBride and Flying Wolf faced me. McBride's sword was drawn and ready. Apple trees rose behind him. Trees that shaded an Ancient Warrior's grave.

Flying Wolf shouted, "Run, white boy!"

Daniel didn't move. Wikbi cawed. He circled overhead, black wings against a hazy sky.

"This American's of no use to anyone!" Flying Wolf cried. "Look at him."

Daniel looked small. The meadow so large. Voices thundered all around him. The smoke from Colonel Butler's army darkened the sky.

"He's nothing but a coward!" Flying Wolf shrieked. "He deserves to die!" Sunlight burned off an upraised sword. McBride stared at me.

"Daniel's no coward!" I shouted back through smoke and anger. "He's my friend!"

A gust of air brought me Daniel's words: "Your closest friend." He stumbled forward into Spotted Owl's descending club. I knew Daniel did this, not for himself, but for me. He ducked beneath Much Talk's flicking branch, then gathered himself and ran past White Fawn and my mother. Red Wing whacked his arm with the flat side of her hoe, but Daniel didn't falter. He ran on through the blows of clubs and switches—until Bad Shoes raised his sharpened hatchet. Daniel's eyes widened. Covering his head with his hands, he slowed. Would he stop? But he mustn't stop! The hatchet blade might turn.

"Daniel!" I screamed silently.

Bad Shoes's hatchet grazed his shoulder, sending Daniel stumbling sideways. Flying Wolf raised his axe. The blade was turned. Daniel floundered toward it as if in a daze.

"No!" I shouted. "No!" And I found myself standing next to my friend, in the middle of the gauntlet, only five strides from the painted post. Our upraised hands were fending off Flying Wolf's descending axe. People everywhere were shouting, "Get out, Coshmoo! Let the white boy face the gauntlet alone! You do not belong!"

I do, I thought. *I do.*

We wrenched the axe from Flying Wolf and threw it on the ground. Daniel's shoulder was badly gashed. His leg was bleeding. But he had run; he had survived. Brave Daniel, I thought, to have come this far.

Wikbi shrieked. A shadow crossed my face. Flying Wolf had retrieved the axe and was slowly raising it again. There was a crazed look in my cousin's eyes.

Time was a river that, for a moment, stopped flowing. Flying Wolf drew a breath, ready to bring the axe back down. I stood beside Daniel. Neither of us moved.

My cousin gave the death halloo. Someone laughed. McBride. His sword sang out. It caught Flying Wolf's descending axe at the angle between its head and its handle. The axe somersaulted through the air and landed at Elk Hair's feet.

Stunned, I looked at Daniel. Stunned, he looked at me. Then a strange song filled his eyes. A happy, triumphant song. McBride grabbed Daniel's shoulder. He yanked, then pushed him to the painted post. He made Daniel take hold of it with both of his hands. "The boy showed courage," McBride shouted to everyone. "He faced your gauntlet. I was the one who captured him—now his fate is mine to decide."

Flying Wolf reached for the axe, his shoulders stiff with anger. Would he defy McBride? Big Nose? He Who Runs with the Wind? No, he dare not. There was so much between them.

"Two dogs. Two frightened dogs. That's what you are," Flying Wolf hissed at Daniel and me.

"No!" my mother said. With impassive faces, Broken Stone and Red Hawk flanked her. "One day these boys will lead their people." Such fierce pride was in her voice. At that moment, I saw within her eyes a mix of overwhelming love and sadness. She touched her cross and stared at something over my left shoulder—a British flag someone had hoisted above our cabin.

McBride took Daniel away that day. I don't know where he took him. Maybe to a Mohawk village. Maybe even farther north. I hoped they climbed Carantouan before they left. I hoped they found an uprooted locust. An empty grave. I never saw my friend again. Not in the way that I see you now, sitting here and breathing. But I've known Daniel's spirit longer than the life of any man. This spirit tells me that the white man with the strange tattoo, sensing perhaps that a quest had ended, eventually set Daniel free.

At dusk, I found White Fawn by the river. She stood near the brush pile where once I'd given her two gifts. Wikbi perched on her shoulder. I was troubled. Daniel was gone. Many in my village were angry over what I'd done—entering a gauntlet to save a settler. A white boy. I needed the stroke of Wikbi's beak along my cheek. But now, as I look back, I can see his wisdom. Wikbi was preparing me.

White Fawn looked so sad. She stared at the setting sun's reflection. The smoke from Colonel Butler's fires clouded the sky across the river. Flying Wolf was there. Gazing at the river, I thought, I'll never escape my cousin or this white man's war.

"White Fawn, when you look at this river, what do you see?" I asked softly, half expecting her to say, "Blue glass beads. Shimmering gold cloth. A black stallion and a snake tattoo."

What she said uplifted me. "Why, Coshmoo, I see . . . pink shells tumbling through sunlight. Silver shad. And boys facing a gauntlet. Two boys, running free."

EPILOGUE

I must end my story now. It is growing dark. Night comes early at the time of falling leaves. It turns happy rocks to shadows. Makes skeletons of trees. It is time for you to go.

Don't point to my burned village. Don't allow those questions in your eyes. Rest in the story that I've told—all those dreams. Look up! Dusk paints the sky with rainbows! Go now, before the night wind comes.

You think you are the rainbowed bird who finds the current in a wind and soars? You think that, like the crow, you can brave the fire and still fly free? Listen to a cycle of revenge that never dies? You want to learn my sorrow?

The British Colonel Butler liked the bottles lined up in our window. He picked each one up in his pale, fat hands and turned it back and forth, splashing color on our floor. He spoke quietly to my mother of Chief Teedyuscung and his dreams for a homeland. He said, "Few Americans are left to defend the Wyoming Valley. We will take it easily. The British king will win the war. He doesn't want to harm your people. You would be wise to join his side.

"Our spies tell us that Americans downriver don't trust you. They want to burn your village. But we'll guarantee you land along the Susquehanna until the moon should die. We will always see to your needs."

Our needs.

"As long as trees embrace the sky, we can fashion bows and arrows," my father once had told me. "And even if the sky rains hard, we can hunt."

But the white man's war, not rain clouds, darkened our sky. Our poor arrows were no match for musket balls. My mother's wings gathered close. White men on both sides viewed us with narrowed eyes. We had little ammunition to protect ourselves, and our muskets needed fixing. The British Colonel Butler had more gunsmiths, muskets, powder, lead, and soldiers than our small village had ever seen.

My mother told our assembled elders, "We have no choice."

The seventh wolf, reluctantly, joined in.

Alongside Colonel Butler's army, we built canoes and rafts. The air was hot and still. Mosquitoes whined. I scraped charred wood from a log and remembered the spirit of a crow that sang to me from pine.

We painted our faces red and black for war, but my heart was not in this painting. My heart remembered pictures drawn in a tree.

Before our canoes and rafts descended the Susquehanna toward the Wyoming Valley, the sun turned black the way the·moon had done. My mother raised her arms. She railed against the darkened sky.

The next morning, I boarded the head canoe, my ammunition pouch heavy with British gunpowder and bullets. Wikbi darted from tree to tree. He tailed our scouting party. All day we paddled downriver, watching for signs of the Americans. At dusk, we cornered three men who'd been hoeing corn downriver from the burned remains of Daniel's cabin.

"Check the river near their beached canoe. See if any more Americans are there," a thin-lipped soldier with pale blue eyes told me.

At the riverbank I heard a soft splash, as if someone had slipped into the water. The Susquehanna eddied here—the river, dark and deep. Weeds trapped leaves, moss, branches, logs—made it easy for a man to hide.

I walked out on the large trunk of a fallen tree. The nearby canoe, empty now, rocked gently. I peered into the water, searching for someone hiding in the debris. Willow leaves swirled on the surface of the river where there was no current. Amid the waterlogged branches of the fallen tree, small bubbles rose. I crouched on the tree. I aimed my musket at the bubbles and waited.

Moments passed. I knew that soon the man would surface. He had to breathe. I imagined him the kind of man who'd shoot a chief like Teedyuscung. He'd be a thick-necked white man with small eyes like a pig's.

A screech owl cried. A slow breeze awakened the

hot, sleeping trees. Mist steamed off the river the way it does at twilight. Bubbles formed a trail that snaked through fallen branches. The surface of the water broke. I saw . . . brown hair . . . blue, frightened eyes . . . the bridge of a nose, thin and freckled. It wasn't a man, but a boy.

He sank below the water to where the river beats. I kept my musket trained on him. Wikbi alighted on my shoulder. I remember how he stroked my cheek. For a moment, just a moment, my thoughts slipped away. I sprawled on a sun-baked rock, and Daniel whispered, "If he swims closer, grab his tail."

I should have been listening to brush and trees. Then I would have heard the poke of a rifle through willow leaves behind me. But I was thinking, It's such a little Red Eye.

My eyes should have been a cougar's. Then I would have caught a willow's fluttering. Then I would have seen the one who held the rifle. Then I would have killed this man before this man killed me.

I didn't feel the bullet. I felt no pain. Only the warmth of arms. Misty arms rising off the river. My father. Teedyuscung. The Ancient Warrior. Daniel. All their arms enfolded me. For the moment, bound together with them, spinning, I felt a holy peace.

The pain came one night later. Pain sharper than the crack of musket fire as Colonel Butler's army devoured American lives upon the Wyoming Valley plain. Pain deeper than the wounds their sabers made. Pain as agonizing as a fire that blackens feathers.

It came as I floated down the Susquehanna. The panting air grew dark. I heard a mother's wail. I saw my mother raise a stone maul against the Wyoming Valley sky. Standing over a moccasin-shaped rock, a circle of white captives surrounding her, my mother cried, "Ten white men's lives for the life of my beloved son. My Coshmoo."

I do not walk the ghostly path that leads to Assowajame, the land beyond my sight. A reeling sorrow roots me here. Look into the valley. See those charred remains? Once that was my village. My village was finer than any white man's town.

From this perch, I watched an American army destroy our corn, squash, cattle, canoes, cabins, ancient graves, and apple trees. I heard their cry, "A hundred Indian villages, a hundred thousand Indian lives for those deaths at Wyoming."

Tell me. Is it wrong to dream?

HISTORICAL NOTE

Queen Esther, a woman known for her friendship with white settlers during the early years of the American Revolution, governed a group of Delawares living near Tioga Point (present-day Athens), Pennsylvania. She had a son who was killed just before the Wyoming Valley massacre, in which, on July 3, 1778, three hundred American patriots were defeated by eleven hundred British, Tories, and Native Americans. Historical accounts vary, but legend has it that Queen Esther was the woman who wielded a stone maul against American captives at what later became known as "The Bloody Rock." The preceding work of historical fiction is an attempt to explain what might have led her to this act.

SELECTED
BIBLIOGRAPHY

Axtell, James. *The Indian Peoples of Eastern America.* New York and Oxford: Oxford University Press, 1981.

Donehoo, George P. *A History of the Indian Villages and Place Names in Pennsylvania.* Harrisburg, PA: Telegraph Press, 1928.

Furlow, John. "Indian Queen of the Wyoming Valley," *Pennsylvania Heritage* 3 (June 1977), pp. 16–19.

Graymont, Barbara. *The Iroquois in the American Revolution.* Syracuse, NY: Syracuse University Press, 1972.

Grumet, Robert S. *The Lenapes.* New York and Philadelphia: Chelsea House, 1989.

Harrington, M. R. *Religion and Ceremonies of the Lenape* (*Indian Notes and Monographs* 19). New York: Museum of the American Indian, Hey Foundation, 1921.

Hayden, Horace Edwin. "Echoes of the Massacre of Wyoming, Number Three: Queen Esther and Joseph Elliott. Was Queen Esther at the Massacre?" *Wyoming Historical and Geological Proceedings* 13 (1914), pp. 124–130.

Heckewelder, John. *History, Manners, and Customs of the Indian Nations Who Once Inhabited Pennsylvania and the Neighboring States* (reprinted from a copy in the State Historical Society of Wisconsin Library). New York: Arno Press and *The New York Times*, 1971.

Johnson, F. C., ed. *The Historical Record: A Quarterly Publication Devoted Principally to the Early History of the Wyoming Valley* 3 (1897).

Kraft, Herbert C. *The Lenape: Archaeology, History, and Ethnography.* Newark, NJ: New Jersey Historical Society, 1986.

Miner, Charles. *A History of Wyoming in a Series of Letters, from Charles Miner, to His Son William Penn Miner Esquire.* Philadelphia: J. Crissy, 1845.

Murray, Elsie. "Esther Montour in Pennsylvania Folklore," *Northumberland County Historical Society Proceedings* 22 (1958), pp. 44–60.

———. *Te-a-o-ga: Annals of a Valley.* Athens, PA: Tioga Point Museum, 1939.

Murray, Louise. *A History of Old Tioga Point and Early Athens, Pennsylvania.* Wilkes-Barre, PA: Raeder Press, 1907.

"Narrative of the Captivity of Mrs. Whittaker, Daughter of Sebastian Strope, A Revolutionary Soldier," *The Quarterly Journal of the New York State Historical Association* 11, no. 3 (July 1930), pp. 237–251.

Newcomb, William W., Jr. *The Culture and Acculturation of the Delaware Indians.* Ann Arbor: University of Michigan Press, 1956.

Peck, George D. D. *Wyoming: Its History, Stirring Incidents, and Romantic Adventures.* New York: Harper & Brothers, 1858.

Perkins, Mrs. George A. *Early Times on the Susquehanna.* Binghamton, NY: Matelle & Reid, 1870.

Sandoz, Mari. *The Beaver Men: Spearheads of Empire.* New York: Hastings House, 1964.

Thompson, Bill. "Lenape Tales," *The Pennsylvania Germans and the Lenape (Delaware Indians): The Period of Contact 1720–1775* (cassette recording of papers given at the annual meeting of the Pennsylvania German Society, April 28–29, 1989, Jordan United Church of Christ, Allentown, PA).

Wallace, Anthony F. C. *King of the Delawares: Teedyuscung, 1700–1763.* Syracuse, NY: Syracuse University Press, 1949, 1990.

Wallace, Paul A. *Indians in Pennsylvania.* Harrisburg, PA: Pennsylvania Historic & Museum Commission, 1970.

———. *Indian Paths of Pennsylvania.* Harrisburg, PA: Pennsylvania Historic & Museum Commission, 1971.

———, ed. *The Travels of John Heckewelder in Frontier America.* Pittsburgh: University of Pittsburgh Press, 1958.

Weslager, C. A. *The Delaware Indians: A History.* New Brunswick, NJ, and London: Rutgers University Press, 1989.

White, Jon. *Everyday Life of the North American Indian.* New York: Holmes & Meier, 1979.